FROM THE
ASHES OF GLORY

HOWARD GOODE

iUniverse, Inc.
Bloomington

From the Ashes of Glory

iUniverse books may be ordered through booksellers or by contacting:

iUniverse
1663 Liberty Drive
Bloomington, IN 47403
www.iuniverse.com
1-800-Authors (1-800-288-4677)

ISBN: 978-1-4620-2064-5 (sc)
ISBN: 978-1-4620-2065-2 (hc)
ISBN: 978-1-4620-2063-8 (e)

Library of Congress Control Number: 2011907712

Printed in the United States of America

iUniverse rev. date: 05/11/2011

CHAPTER 1

Someone once said that the only absolute constant in life is change itself. As fate would have it, politics entered the picture in the late 1850s, and the tranquil South would be changed forever.

Oakmont was one of the grandest plantations in central Tennessee. The two thousand acres produced a variety of food products, such as grain, cattle, and hogs. Oakmont also produced some of the finest thoroughbred horses found anywhere in Tennessee.

The main house, a Greek Revival, stood impressively on a small knoll and was surrounded by an old stand of giant oaks. The two-story front gallery ran the full width of the house. The gallery roof was supported by six Corinthian columns, and the front of the house displayed a dozen floor-length windows, three on either side at both levels. Over the massive carved front door was a fanlight window, designed to allow extra daylight into the wide hallway that served the downstairs rooms. There were twelve large rooms to the house, six on each level, plus a servant's quarters that was located at the rear of the house and attached only by a covered walkway.

John Newton, the owner of Oakmont, was known throughout the area as a very successful planter, and was held in high regard by the citizens of Maury County, Tennessee. Neighbors had always dropped by Oakmont to discuss current event or to ask John's opinion. By early summer of 1860, the visits had become more numerous, and the talk became increasingly more solemn. Rumors of a possible war between the North and the South spread rampant over the land, and a fearful anticipation crept over Tennessee like storm clouds approaching over the horizon.

Morgan Montgomery came to Oakwood to live as a nine-year-old orphan, brought there by his mother's relatives, John and Martha Newton. Now seventeen years old, Morgan was only interested in helping run the large plantation, attending classes at Jackson College in nearby Columbia Tennessee, and when time permitted, a little hunting and fishing with his friends. He had little interest in the politics of the day until John Newton suggested that he start attending the meetings that John frequently held in their home.

In late July, word was passed throughout the area that a meeting would take place at Oakmont on the following Saturday afternoon. Almost every white adult male for miles around attended. Martha Newton didn't mind the more genteel of the neighbors gathering in her parlor, but when the caucus became a crowd, John adjourned to the shade of the oak grove in the side yard. The servants brought out chairs and benches, which were given to the older gentlemen, while most of the more than one hundred men seated themselves on the grass or simply leaned against nearby trees. John stood near the top of the steps that ascended to the high side porch and spoke first.

"My good friends and neighbors, it is with pleasure that I welcome you all to Oakmont. It's very reassuring to me that so many of you have taken the time to come together to discuss some very important issues. I refer, of course, to the political upheaval this nation is experiencing, and the things that are taking place around the country that directly pertain to each and every one of us gathered here today. For those of you who have been able to stay abreast of the happenings around the country, I will only endeavor to refresh your memory. And for those of you who are not completely aware of the threatening political trends—trends that could directly, and perhaps adversely, effect the South—let me present the latest news that I have been able to assimilate."

There was a brief distraction as several of the men stopped talking among themselves and moved closer to better hear. "As most of you already know, the Republican Party has picked Mister Abraham Lincoln to be their candidate in the upcoming presidential election. I'm sorry to report to you that the Democratic Party has split into two factions—which, I should add, will help put Mister Lincoln into the White House. One faction, the Northern Democrats, has nominated Senator Douglas for President. The other faction, mostly Southern, has chosen Vice President Breckinridge as their man, and now a group of distinguished gentlemen from the South has formed a fourth political party, which they call the Constitutional Union Party."

Someone in the crowd yelled, "Yeah, Yeah, Yeah."

John paused a moment before continuing. "They have offered former Senator John Bell, from our own state of Tennessee, to be their man in the race. Now, gentlemen, as many of us have discussed in some of our previous meetings, the Northern states have nearly two-thirds of the electoral votes. Not all the Northern vote will go to Lincoln, but most will. I am sure that Senator Douglas will get the remainder of the Northern vote, but due to the fact that his party has split, I don't believe that he stands a chance of being elected. Even if he were to defeat Lincoln, it would not benefit the South, because, in my humble opinion he would be more of an enemy to the South than would Lincoln."

John stopped speaking for a moment to let his words sink. "The election of either of these gentlemen will destroy the South as we know it and forever change our way of life, because there will be a division of this great nation. And that division could, and most likely will, lead to bloodshed. As many of you well know, the issue of slavery is not the only dispute between us and the North, but the North will tell the world that all the conflict between our two regions has been brought about because of slavery. The world needs the food and fiber that we produce, but my friends, the North, under either Mister Lincoln or Mister Douglas, can turn the world away from our door and close those markets."

Murmuring could be heard from among the group as some of the men made comments to those around them.

"There is talk throughout the South of secession, or withdrawing from the Union," John said. "Word has come to me that four or five of our sister states are making plans to secede if Lincoln is elected. Tennessee could well follow. We as a nation have twice defeated the great armies of the British. Throughout the world we are respected as a power with which to be reckoned. We have won great battles and gained the world's respect, not because we are many states, but because all the states present themselves as one nation."

"Here, here," someone called out from the back of the crowd.

But someone else yelled, "That sounds like a lot of hogwash to me."

Paying no heed to the interruptions, John proceeded. "The greatest leader the world has ever known once said, 'Every kingdom divided against itself is brought to desolation, and every city or house divided against itself shall not stand.' Gentlemen, I am opposed to any division of these United States. If the Southern states were to secede and become an independent nation, what is to prevent two or three of those states from later becoming disgruntled and pulling out of that union, thus further dividing and weakening the South, and America? In my opinion we should do all in our power to remain one nation under God."

At that point muttering and noisy conversations could be heard from different locations within the crowd.

"As I have said, there are many serious issues other than slavery being used to fan the hot embers of animosity, further driving a wedge between us and our Northern neighbors. There is one significantly important issue that we can begin to resolve, and I should add there is all likelihood that someday we could be forced to do so. That issue, my friends, is slavery."

During the last few minutes there had been much clearing of throats, coughing, and fidgeting around. A few men in the crowd were clearly unhappy with John's last statements. Although he had not finished speaking, one man shouted back to him, "You're a fine one to talk like that. You own more slaves than just 'bout any of us here. What do you plan to do with yours? Turn 'em loose and tell 'em you don't need 'em anymore?"

John waited until the crowed settled down a little before replying. "That is a reasonable question, and I'll try to give a reasonable answer. As many of you know, I have in the last few years changed my opinion and attitude about slavery. Many of my hands are now free men; they are still given food and lodging, but they are paid modest wages to work my crops. The ones who are still bound to me under the rights of ownership are being credited with equal wages for their labor. And at such time as those credits equal my original investment in the individual slave, that slave is given papers of freedom. I have done this with many of my former slaves, and I plan to do it with each and every Negro who is still indentured to me."

Some of the men in the crowd began to shout angrily. There were yells of, "I'll not stay here and listen to that kind of fool talk," and, "We ought to run him out of Maury County." One man threw a horse muffin, which narrowly missed John. At that point Manford Smith, the sheriff of Maury County, pulled his pistol and fired two shots into the air, after which he yelled for everyone to settle down and be quiet. About two dozen men left, and there was much loud discourse among those who remained.

Randolph Watkins, one of Columbia's leading citizens, climbed up onto the step beside John and raised his voice, "Gentlemen,

gentlemen! John Newton has been a friend and neighbor to all of us for many years. He is a wise and good man, and most important, he is our host. Let us all show our good breeding and hear him out."

The noise subsided a little, and John said, "Thank you, Randolph and Manford. To all of you other gentlemen, the day will come, sooner or later, when we will have to consider working our farms and plantations without slave labor. What I'm doing about my slaves is my business and my business alone. It may not be sound business, and it may not be in the best interest of Oakmont, but it is what my conscience dictates, and I can no longer consider myself a righteous man if I continue to act against my conscience."

Again there was much moving around and murmuring throughout the remaining crowd, with an occasional loud shout. John stood silent until the noise subsided once more.

"Gentlemen, I've tried to make two points today: One is that we need to think long and hard about what's happening to our nation before we become so complacent as to stand by and allow it to be divided. Also, I felt compelled to tell you what I'm doing to get out of a wrongful practice, and in a way that will help offset some of my losses of capital investment."

"I will say one more thing, just so the ones of you who don't really know me won't think me a complete traitor to my people. Have no doubt about it—I am a Southerner, now and forever. If war does come, and I do believe it will, I shall have to fight, in whatever way and with whatever means available to me, on the side of the South. But the very thought of war saddens me deeply. Thank you for your indulgence."

There were other speakers, some partially agreeing with John, but most disagreed and at times openly criticized much of what he had said.

*   *   *

Hours later, after all participates had left, Morgan knocked at the door of John's study. John invited him in and asked what was on his mind. "I hear all of these people talking," Morgan said, "but I'm not sure I understand what's going on. In fact, I get the feeling, based on some of the conversations I've heard, that many of our neighbors are about as confused as I. Why is there so much quarreling with the Northern politicians, and to what is it leading?"

"My boy, you've asked two intelligent questions that do not lend themselves to short answers. As I said in my speech, slavery is an important issue, but it is definitely not the root issue dividing the North and the South. There is a sectional division, or geographical difference between the North and South, going back to colonial times."

"I guess I've never realized that we had any major differenced with the North," Morgan said, "but I'm sorry for the interruption, sir. Please continue."

"That's okay, Morgan; I want you to ask questions. It's important that you understand what we are facing. A favorable climate and good soil helped establish a rural way of life in the South, supported by an agricultural economy. The cooler climate gave the Northerners a short growing seasons, and much of the soil is not as fertile as that found in the South, which made establishing of large farming operations less practical in the North. Their economy came to depend more on trade and bartering than on agriculture, which led to the development of industry and commerce.

"Their lifestyles and attitudes are totally different from ours. They are, for the most part, descendants of the old Puritan stock from Plymouth Rock. We Southerners come from the proud and aristocratic stock of Cavaliers. Few Northerners have achieved the peace of mind and contentment that so many Southerners enjoy. The

Northerner looks to the future for a better way of life, whereas we are proud of the past and pleased with the present."

"This is very interesting. I learned a lot of this in school, but I didn't consider it very important at the time," Morgan interjected.

"Our history is very important, my boy. We can better plan our future of we know what and why things have happened in our past."

At that time one of the servants came into the room with coffee. John thanked the servant and then continued the conversation with Morgan.

"The United States Congress, of which the majority of its members are elected by the Northern vote, has over the past few years enacted many laws that favor the Northerner and punish the Southerner—things like import taxes on the things needed in the South and export tariffs on the South's agriculture products. They have allocated money for improving transportation in the North while spending very little for the same purpose in the South. There is also the controversy between the federal government and the Southern states over what rights and powers the states possess. I am definitely in agreement with most Southerners on this matter."

"Can you explain to me what rights each state should have?" Morgan asked.

"I'll simplify my ideals concerning states' rights for brevity's sake. Each state should have the right to determine what and how things are done within that state. The federal government was originally established to provide national protection and to enact such laws, and impose such taxes and tariffs as are necessary for dealing with other countries. Many Southerners believe that the federal government is already trying to exert control over the individual state by using the might and power given by the constitution for the sole purpose of protecting its citizens against aggression from other countries.

"You didn't say much about states' rights to the others today; do you think most of them feel the same way you do?"

"Morgan, I didn't dare share all of my predictions with the crowd today. Many of them weren't ready." John then paused while he got up from his overstuffed leather chair and walked over and opened one of the tall six-foot windows. There had been a shower of rain soon after the crowd left, and one of the servants had closed all the windows, but John wanted the fresh air. "Why so many of these people prefer to remain uninformed about things that will greatly affect their future is beyond me." He paused again to pour coffee and pondered what he had just said. "Based on all the news and information that I've been able to assimilate in the past few months, I predict that Mister Lincoln will win the election by a landslide. When this happens, most of the South will try to secede from the Union, and Lincoln will not and cannot allow that to happen. War will come. It will be a short but a bloody conflict. The South will lose."

Many of John Newton's predictions came true. Abraham Lincoln was elected president; he received 180 electoral votes while Breckinridge received 72. Bell, the Tennessean, received 39 votes, and Douglas, who had bragged that he could defeat Abraham Lincoln any day of the week, came in far behind with only 11 of the 302 electoral votes.

Before Lincoln could be inaugurated, the Union started to fall apart. On December 20, 1860, South Carolina passed its Ordinance of Secession, which declared the Union dissolved as far as South Carolina was concerned. The following January five other states—Mississippi, Florida, Alabama, Georgia, and Louisiana—followed South Carolina. In February, the six rebelling states sent representatives to Montgomery, Alabama, and formed the

Confederate States of America. Jefferson Davis of Mississippi was elected president, and Alexander Stephens of Georgia would serve as vice president.

Only two days before Lincoln was inaugurated, on March 2, 1861, Texas joined the Confederacy. On April 12, 1861, an event took place that would change the South and the nation forever. Confederate cannons fired on Fort Sumter, a small military post in Charleston Harbor, South Carolina. The fort surrendered the next day and was then occupied by the Southerners. Two days later Lincoln ordered Union forces to proceed to Charleston and recapture it. The South considered this—and not what they had done three days earlier—a declaration of war. Soon Virginia, Arkansas, and North Carolina joined the Confederacy. As John Newton had predicted, Tennessee joined the rest of the South. John was only wrong on one part of his prediction: the war would not be short-lived.

On April 27, Lincoln proclaimed a blockade of all Southern ports. In May, the leaders of the Confederacy made Richmond, Virginia, their capital. Both North and South sent out calls for volunteers, with each side receiving more men than could be equipped. By July, the Union had assembled a large army near Washington, and the South positioned an equally large force across the Potomac River in Virginia. The war that would pit state against state, friend against friend, and brother against brother had truly begun.

We are a band of brothers and native to the soil,
Fighting for the property we gained by honest toil;
And when our rights were threatened, the cry rose near and far,
"Hurrah for the Bonnie Blue Flag that bears a single star!"
Hurrah! Hurrah! For Southern rights hurrah!
Hurrah for the Bonnie Blue Flag that bears a single star.
Harry McCarthy, "The Bonnie Blue Flag"

CHAPTER 2

Most of the able-bodied young men of Maury County joined together to formed Company H, which became attached to the First Regiment, Tennessee Volunteers. They referred to themselves as The Maury Grays. Mothers, wives, sisters, and sweethearts worked tirelessly to make handsome uniforms for their brave loved ones who were off to the war. The uniforms consisted of an eight-button medium gray frock coat with a black standing collar and plain cuffs. The pants were medium gray with a two-inch black stripe down the outer seams. The hats were black with a light colored plume. Morgan thought his friends were very dapper and debonair in their new uniforms. He was now six feet tall with an athletic physique and was sure he wood look good in on of the fine uniforms.

After most of Morgan's friends had gone away to camp, he was not at all content to stay in Maury County and help manage Oakmont, but he reluctantly agreed with John's opinion that the South needed the food that Oakmont could produce. He often found himself considering his options and yearning to enlist, but each time he forced those thoughts and yearnings from his mind.

News of the war was scant, but from time to time Oakmont received word of battles in which the Maury Grays had fought. In late February of 1862, Morgan's conversation with an overnight guest at Oakmont caused his greatest trepidation. Colonel Nathan

Bedford Forrest, an old friend of John's, stopped at Oakmont to visit and spend the night while his cavalry camped along a nearby stream.

After supper was over, the men, including Morgan, adjourned to John's study. After a fine meal followed by a good smoke and a few queries from John, the colonel seemed more than willing to tell his version of the battle of Donelson, in which he had recently been engaged. After lighting a cigar from the box John had presented to him as a gift, Colonel Forrest related his personal observations and analysis of the fighting. Everyone around Columbia had heard reports about how Grant's troops had captured the river fort a few days earlier. Some rumors said the fort was given up without a fight, and others had the Southerners holding on until the last man was down. Now Morgan was in the company of a man who had actually participated in the battle for the fort, and the young man's emotions were deeply stirred as Forrest began to tell his story.

"I do believe that with some good generalship we could have held Fort Donelson," Forrest began, "although it's true that we were outmanned and outgunned. I guess our trouble really started when General Tilghman gave up Fort Henry with little or no fight. He took his men and skedaddled to Fort Donelson, with the Yanks right on his tail. Me and my men were bivouacked over at Mason Crossroad when a messenger rode into camp with orders. I was to rush over to Donelson with my cavalry to support General Pillow, which I promptly did. Pillow was doin' a tolerable good job runnin' things until two more generals, Floyd and Buckner, showed up, with each one wantin' to be the bell cow.

"Floyd allowed as how he was senior officer and took command. The first words out of that man's mouth were orders for us to get ready to abandon the fort. Pillow was able to talk some sense into his thick head and change his mind, but only for the time bein'. As I said before, we were outmanned and outgunned, but we made a good stand. We fought from inside and outside the fort. Several times my cavalry charged out through enemy lines and back again, killing a passel of their men and capturing a bunch of their arms and supplies. During one such affray, my men killed over two hundred Yankees and captured six cannons. That time we lost eighteen men, wounded or captured, and two horses. It happened that I was riding both them horses, one at a time, of course. I don't have a lot of luck with horses; to this day I've had six animals shot right out from under me.

"Anyway, Old Grant couldn't make much headway against us on the ground, and so he had Commodore Foote, head of the Yankee navy, bring several gunboats up the river and anchor just out of our cannon range. On the fourteenth, the boats moved in a little closer, and their gunners opened fire on our battery, which was dug in along the river. Then word went around that he was sending us a Valentine message, and so our cannoneers, wantin' to be proper and polite, sent one right back. I reckon he planned to move even closer and hit the fort after he knocked out the river battery, but our men made him skedaddle back down the river, under a full head of steam. Of course, a few of their boats was damaged so bad they had to drift back down river. Old Foote caused a lot of damage, but we caused a lot more to him."

Forrest stopped speaking when a servant came in, bringing cups and a pot of steaming coffee on a tray. As Morgan poured a cup for Forrest, the colonel remarked, "Haven't had a cup of good coffee in days." After a few sips he said, "Morgan, I sure hope I'm not boring you to death."

"Oh, no, sir! I could listen all night. And I'm pleased to have you as a guest in our home," Morgan answered.

"Well, thank you, my boy. You know, John Newton and I go back a long ways. We've done some business together from time to time during the last several years, and he's been in my home in Memphis on several occasions."

Morgan wanted to hear more about the fighting and asked, "Sir, would you tell me how Grant managed to capture Fort Donelson if our boys were doing so well?"

After taking another long sip of coffee and relighting his half-smoked cigar, Forrest replied, "Yes, our boys did fight well, and the answer to your question is short and simple. Grant was able to take the fort because our commanding general gave it to him. He wouldn't listen to nobody, paid no heed to reports on the enemy's strength and positions—even when we'd risked life and limb to get the information. On the night of the fifteenth, a bugle call summoned all officers to report to the commander. I arrived a little late, and the first thing I heard out of General Floyd's mouth was him telling about his plan to surrender the fort. We'd been through that before, but this time there was no way to separate him from his fool notion. He said that Grant had us surrounded, and it would be honorable to surrender under such conditions. And to try to sweeten that sour notion, he added that he would be doing it to save our boys. To save our generals was what I thought he was really sayin'.

"There was a lot of arguing back and forth among the officers, but pretty soon it was a sure thing that we would be giving up the fort."

At that point, Forrest stood up, walked over the coffee pot, and poured himself more coffee. After returning to his chair, he continued with his story. "There was only one fly in Floyd's ointment: he didn't want it goin' on his record that he surrendered. So he turned the command over to General Buckner. When the dust settled, I pulled Buckner off to one side and said to him that if we was gonna do such a stupid thing, would he please allow me to get my men out first. I told him I thought we could break through their lines if we charged hard and fast. After a bit of contention, he agreed to let me try it. I immediately rushed out to get my men ready. In ten minutes we was in the saddle. I've got to say that luck rode with us. We happened upon a weak spot in the Yankee lines and got clean away without the loss of a single man or horse.

"When we had traveled a safe distance from Donelson, we stopped to rest our horses. Then an hour later, we headed out to Nashville. Well, wouldn't you know, when we got there the town was also falling to the Yankees. We had to turn tail and run again. We've now been ordered to Huntsville, Alabama, which is where I'm a-headin'." Forrest finished out the evening by telling stories of some of the other battles and skirmishes in which he had participated.

As the colonel prepared to leave the next morning, he called Morgan off to the side. "Morgan, John told me how he needs you here, but we need all the fightin' men we can get, and I'd be proud to have you in my unit. If you ever decide that's what you want, just come a-ridin'."

Needless to say, Morgan slept very little for several nights thereafter. He had seen so many of his friends go into service, and for months he had strongly felt that he too should be serving with them. After Forrest's visit, his yearning to enlist became so strong that he was not sure he could contain it much longer. His frustration was obvious to others. One evening after supper, John asked him, "What's troubling you, my boy? You've been off your feed for days. Is there anything you'd like to talk about?"

"Yes, sir, I guess there is," answered Morgan. "I've been thinking a lot about something I need to say, but now it's hard to find the words."

"Let me help you," John kindly interrupted. "You want to enlist."

"Yes, sir, I do. Everyone my age has already joined up, some even younger. You know that Sam Watkins and just about all of my friends enlisted more than a year ago, when they formed the Maury

Grays. Jennie Mayes had a letter from Sam with her at church last Sunday, and she let me read it. There were two pages telling about being in the battle of Shiloh. Then he wanted to know if I was still at home. I know how you need me here, but I'm really beginning to feel like a slacker."

"I certainly can't think of you as a slacker, and I doubt if any of your friends think so. We do need you here, and the South needs the things you can help provide by staying here. But only you can make the final decision."

CHAPTER 3

Time passed slowly for Morgan, although he took on more of the duties and responsibilities of managing Oakmont than he previously had. He also threw himself into much of the physical labor, caring for the many farm animals and working long hours with the field hands. He tried to be content with the fact that he was helping produce food for the South, but he was unable to suppress his aspirations of becoming a soldier.

In February of 1863, he decided that he could no longer stay out of the fighting. Events just prior to that time caused him to finally make the decision to enlist. During the last days of December and the first days of January, the armies of the North and South clashed in the Battle of Stones River, at Murfreesboro, which was less than fifty miles from Oakmont. Two of Morgan's friends, Mark Harper and Tommy Belton, were killed in the battle, and several other members of the Maury Grays were wounded. After the battle, the company was pulled back for rest and to find necessary replacements for the dead and wounded.

Sam Watkins had been shot in the arm, and he took what he referred to as "French Leave" and came to Columbia to see his sweetheart, Jennie. Early one evening, Morgan saddled his horse and rode into town to find a copy of the latest newspaper. One of the first people he saw was Sam, with one arm in a sling and the other one around Jennie. Morgan asked about the wound, but Sam insisted that it was not serious and he was doing fine. Morgan didn't believe him and thought he was only being modest. He felt concern for Sam, and he had never seen so much physical change in a person in such a short time. Sam had been away less than two years, yet he had aged ten years in appearance, and he was several pounds lighter than the last time Morgan had seen him. Knowing that Sam and Jennie had but a precious few hours to spend together, Morgan talked with Sam only a few minutes before excusing himself.

Later that night Morgan mustered up enough courage to tell John and Martha that he was going to enlist. Martha's chin quivered when she was told, and Morgan could see that she was having a hard time holding back her tears, but he knew she would not allow him to see her cry. "I'm not at all surprised," John said. "I've been rather anxious about this, expecting it for months. I realize how difficult it's been for you, with the fighting going on all around us, and you torn between the duty to stay here and the one to go fight. I'll not try to keep you here any longer. I respect your feelings, and I assure you that neither Martha nor I will have any ill will toward you for going. Just remember, Oakmont is your home. There will always be a place for you here when this terrible conflict is over. All I ask is that you take care of yourself and come back to us as soon as you can."

Morgan spent the next few weeks getting caught up on his duties around Oakmont and organizing everything before his departure. He was both excited and apprehensive about his decision to enlist. Even though he was always very tired at night, he found it difficult to fall asleep at bedtime. When he could not sleep, he would reminisce about all the good times he had enjoyed at Oakmont. One of his most vivid memories was of a Fourth of July horse race in which he had been allowed to ride.

Although John would be riding Pride of Oakmont in the race, he had been reluctant to let Morgan ride for reasons of safety, but at the last minute he had given his consent. Morgan would ride Raven, a beautiful black three-year-old that he had worked with from the time it was a colt. Morgan had gently trained Raven to the saddle and had ridden him for many hours during the past year; he knew everything about the animal.

In his mind, he relived the exuberance and excitement of that day. The large grandstand was full, and people lined the one-mile oval track on both sides. John found Morgan and told him that he estimated the crowd to be more than two thousand people, which did nothing to ease the anxiety that had been building within him since being told that he could enter the race. He purposely stayed busy preparing Raven for the race. He spent the last twenty minutes rubbing Raven with a folded piece of coarse tow cloth. Raven was in a strange place and around unfamiliar animals and people, and Morgan believed that a good rubdown would help relax the animal. At five minutes before race time, Morgan placed the blanket and saddle on Raven and tightened the cinch.

The race master called for the horses to be positioned at the starting line. There were two dozen horses entered in the event, too many for all to line up abreast on the track. There was much bumping and crowding and rough language as riders struggled for a front starting position. A couple of the riders lost control of their mounts. One horse bucked off its rider, and another animal turned and ran the opposite direction from where the race was to take place. As Morgan was forced to the back of the pack, he thought about what John had told him that morning, about how rough a race could become.

Morgan did not have a chance to work his way toward the front before the Race Master fired a pistol into the air, and the race was on. Raven had shot forward like a tightly coiled spring being released. By the time they had gone a quarter of a mile, Raven had passed most of the competitors. Another rider hit Raven across the face with his whip, but the horse was unscathed. Most of the riders used whips on their mounts, but Morgan had refused to even carry one. Only a half dozen of the better horses were now in front of the big black stud. Morgan gave him free rein, allowing him to make his way through the front-runners. As they came around the final curve, less than a quarter of a mile from the finish line, there were only three horses ahead of Raven, and then two. With a final display of courage and stamina, Raven passed another horse, leaving only Pride of Oakmont, John Newton's mount, in front of him. He was only a head behind Pride when they flashed across the finish line.

John and Morgan slowed their horses to a gallop and then to a trot as they continued down the track. When they came to the beginning of the first curve, they turned their mounts around and walked them back toward the winner's circle in front of the big grandstand. "My boy, do you realize that you almost won? I saw what happened to you back there, at the beginning of the race. If you had been given a sportsmanlike start, you and Raven would have beaten the best horse in Maury County."

All Morgan could say was, "Thank you, sir. Thank you for allowing me the chance to race."

Morgan also thought about the circumstances under which he came to Oakmont. His mother had told him many stories about her life in Maury County, and how she had fallen in love with a young man from neighboring Lewis County. After marrying her first love, she joined him on his small farm, which was the home Morgan had known for the first nine years of his life.

He had sad memories of his father, who had preceded his mother in death by three years. In memory he relived the events of his mother's death. John Newton, his mother's relative, and Martha attended the funeral, after which they brought Morgan home with them to live at Oakmont. He had grown to love the Newtons like a child would love his parents, and he knew the feeling was mutual. He knew that the future would be uncertain until the war ended, and he was sad at the thoughts of leaving his home and the people he loved.

Morgan learned from Jennie Mayes that Sam Watkins had returned to his unit the day after Morgan had talked to him. When he got back to camp, he had been court-martialed for being absent without proper furlough. He had been found guilty and given thirty days fatigue duty plus the forfeiture of four months' pay. "French Leave" had been a common occurrence among the soldiers after such a bloody battle as Stones River, and so on the same day as Sam's trial, General Polk had given a blanket pardon to everyone who had returned on his own accord.

Then the day came for Morgan to leave, on February 19, 1863. The previous night he had told John and Martha that he loved them very much and that he was already looking forward to coming back soon. "I'm afraid this war will last much longer than our esteemed politicians are predicting," John said. "Some bragged that we would win in six months, and I too thought it would be short-lived, but we'll soon be into the third year with no end in sight. Morgan, I won't rehash the things we've talked about before, but I believe that conditions will get much worse for all of us before this war ends, and I also believe that the fighting will last much longer. My boy, I think you know what I'm about to say, but I'm going to say it anyway: I love you as much as if you were my own son. I'll pray for you while you're away, and there will be a place for you here when this dreadful is war over. Don't ever forget that this is your home, and it always will be."

Martha was now crying quietly but openly. "Oh, Morgan, I have promised myself a dozen times that I would not cry in front of you, but just look at me now. I don't want you to remember me like this when you are away from home. I want you to remember my happy face." She paused a moment as she blotted the tears from her face with her kerchief and regained her composure. "Son—and you are indeed a son to me—you have become so much a part of my life in these past ten years, and I am having great difficulty in turning loose, but I know the time has come for me to do so. I will pray for you every night, for God's protection, and for a safe return to us."

Sissy, the family cook who had been given her freedom a few years earlier, prepared a fine breakfast for him that morning. The proud little woman had always done a superb job in the kitchen, but that morning she made sure that everything was cooked to perfection. There was smoked ham, red-eye gravy, a heaping plate of flaky biscuits, soft scrambled eggs, several kinds of fruit jellies and preserves, and the always-present pot of steaming coffee.

When she had placed the food on the table, she walked to the kitchen doorway and stood there, watching with pride as Morgan enthusiastically consumed the food. John and Martha had joined him at the table, but neither of them ate; they sat silently while he cleaned his plate a second time. There was little for anyone to say. Everything had been said.

John drove Morgan into Columbia, where he reported to the officer in charge of recruiting. Morgan and seven other men soon boarded a wagon for a three-day trip to Camp Davis, a small, newly built camp near Hornsby, Tennessee. The Maury Grays, along with thousands of other Tennesseans, had trained at Camp Cheatam, near Nashville, but federal troops had destroyed the camp and occupied the surrounding territory.

Of the six other recruits on the wagon, three were young boys who appeared to be no more than fourteen or fifteen years of age, two were near Morgan's age, and the sixth one looked to be more than fifty years old. Morgan learned that the six had come up from an area commonly referred to as the Barrens, in north Lawrence County. All six were blood relatives and all were farmers, except the old man, who was a harness maker. Two cousins to the boys, and nephews to the old man, had been killed in the battle of Stones River, and now the six were going to fight the enemy because they believed it was family duty.

The two nights on the road were almost festive events. Everyone helped in gathering wood for a roaring fire. The wagon driver, who also did the cooking, had brought plenty of good food from the supply depot at Columbia. After supper and extra cups of coffee, the old man from the Barrens would play songs on a homemade banjo he had brought along, and one of the young boys played a mouth organ while the other members of the party sang.

The driver was also a storyteller who enjoyed the attention of his listeners. He told them that he had lost his left foot soon after the war started and had been permanently assigned to light duty. Morgan enjoyed listening to the driver's stories but didn't believe much of what the man told. He claimed to have killed over fifty Yankees during the short time he was active. Morgan didn't think the others believed him either, but everyone listened politely.

Near noon of the second day of travel, they came to the Tennessee River near Clifton. There was a long line of wagons and other horse-drawn vehicles, mostly civilian, waiting to cross on the ferry. The ferry operator moved the civilian traffic aside and took the military first. This caused a lot of grumbling from those who had to wait, but Morgan and his companions were glad to get to the other side and find a campsite before dark.

The rest of the trip was uneventful, and by noon of the third day they arrived at Camp Davis. There they would spend the next several weeks in intense training.

*   *   *

While the new Tennessee recruits underwent a very rigorous training schedule at Camp Davis, events occurred around the country directly affected the future of both North and South. One of the most militarily strategic locations in the South was Vicksburg, Mississippi. The town of a little more than five thousand staunchly Confederate inhabitants stood on a two-hundred-foot bluff on the eastern bank of the Mississippi River. This made the perfect location from which to stop the enemy's river traffic. Having access to transportation along the Mississippi was vitally important to both the North and the South. In Washington, Abraham Lincoln looked at a map and commented to those around him, "See what a lot of land these fellows hold, of which Vicksburg is the key … Let us get Vicksburg and all the country is ours. The war can never be brought to a close until that key is in our pocket."

The Union leaders planned a new battle front that would have as its primary objective the siege, capture, and occupation of Vicksburg. Grant soon headed for Mississippi with every man, horse, and piece of military hardware he could muster.

CHAPTER 4

Although Morgan had requested assignment to a cavalry unit, he and the several hundred other Tennessee recruits were trained for the infantry. Morgan wasn't sure he would ever become accustomed to the mud, the dirt, and the infantry clothes that were issued to him. The uniforms were made of heavy, scratchy wool and were at best ill fitting. He was, however, allowed to wear the wide-brimmed felt hat and comfortable shoes that he had brought from home.

At the end of each day, he would be so tired that he would fall asleep as soon as he stretched out on his less-than-comfortable cot, which consisted of a thin feather mattress supported by ropes attached to a wooden frame. At night he dreamed of marching through mud, firing his musket by the hour, and never-ending drill commands—right oblique, left oblique, guide center, close up, double quick, fire at will.

Weeks of arduous training were followed by another week of waiting for duty assignment, while the decision could be made as to where they were needed the most. One morning, word came that Grant was in Jackson, Tennessee, heading for Bolivar, which was only ten miles from Camp Davis. Everyone was ordered out of camp, with men disbursing in every direction. Five hundred men, including Morgan, were ordered to strike tents and place everything on board waiting wagons for a trip to Jackson, Mississippi.

*   *   *

The nearly three hundred miles took most of nine days to travel by foot. There had been several days of rain, and the roads were soft and muddy, almost impassable for the freight wagons that accompanied them. The mud-covered recruits had to continually help the bogged-down wagons. Several times riders came to bring messages to the commending officer, and they were eventually told that their mission was to reinforce and ultimately replace the garrison assigned to guard the supply depots located around Jackson.

Upon arriving in Jackson, the unit, which had not yet been given a name, made camp and moved into a loosely organized routine of military life. Among the thousands of soldiers bivouacked around Jackson were men from most of the Southern states. But as far as Morgan could determine, the only Tennesseans were the ones who had come with him from Camp Davis. Day and night there was always a beehive of activity around Jackson, with a constant flow of men and equipment moving in and out of the area. There were horses by the thousands, some tethered and some in rope corrals. Wagons and light transport vehicles parked in every available space.

Although the weather remained cold for that time of year, and downpours of rain came daily, flies were so numerous that Morgan found it difficult to keep the pesky insects off of his food while trying to eat. There was also the distinct odor from hundreds of horses around the camps. There was also the noise of the horses, the whinnying, nickering, and continuous stomping of feet. Mixed with those sounds were the ever-present rattling and squeaking of wheeled vehicles moving in and out of the area. Needless to say, there was never a quiet moment for Morgan. He did not regret joining the army, but he missed the tranquility of Oakmont.

The tent that he shared with seven other Tennesseans was located only a few hundred feet from a hospital surgical tent. Surgery, which previously had all been performed during the day, was now being done around the clock. This was the result of the war intensifying as it moved closer to Jackson. The screams of the ill-fated patients would often keep Morgan awake all night. Every night he prayed for the men in the surgical tent, for the war to be over before the entire South drowned in blood.

Unlike the strict military authority that had dictated Morgan's every move back at Camp Davis, there appeared to be little organization and no real chain of command around Jackson. Reports of heavy fighting in central Mississippi were on the increase, but Morgan's commanding officer, Captain Rayford Gentry, was unable to obtain specific orders about where his men were to be deployed. Instead of guarding supply depots, as they had traveled so far to do, the men spent their time reading, writing letters, visiting among the other units, or just sleeping when the noise would allow it.

Things changed, however, before real boredom became a problem. On April 20, Captain Gentry received orders to take his five hundred Tennesseans to Edwards Station, a few miles west of Jackson, to guard a section of the railroad against a marauding unit of Yankee cavalry, commanded by a Colonel Benjamin Grierson. According to the information accompanying the orders, which Captain Gentry read to his unit, Grierson had been sent into Mississippi by Grant to disrupt supply and communication lines, but Grierson's campaign had become one of pillaging and looting. The report further stated that Grierson's raiders had been accused of several counts of murder and rape.

Within the hour, Captain Gentry and his untried young rebels were at the outskirts of Jackson, eagerly marching westward toward a known destination but an unknown destiny. As they went through the little town of Clinton, the local inhabitants cheered for them. As they passed Hillman College, an all girl school, several young ladies threw kisses and flowers at them. Heads were held a little higher and steps were livelier as each man felt a boost of pride and self-esteem.

By three o'clock they had left the main road and following a little-traveled woods road, reaching the railroad. From there they marched westward along the rail bed to Edwards Station. They reached their destination in time to set up camp before dark. The men built cooking fires and spent a mirthful evening, perhaps thinking of the glory and excitement of the skirmish that might soon come their way.

The exuberance waned with the passing of time, but life around camp did not become boring. There was no action but enough hearsay reports reached camp, both from civilians and passing rebel patrols, to keep everyone on the alert. Camp scuttlebutt had it that a large infantry unit from Grant's army was somewhere in the area, and that Grierson was also still on the prowl.

Having always been a little on the impetuous side, Morgan decided he would rather be fighting than forever waiting for the fight. He cleaned his rifle every day, each time remembering the little line he had been required to memorize while in training at Camp Davis. *This is a fifty-eight caliber Enfield rifle-musket, the principal rifle used by the Confederate States of America, costing fourteen dollars and ninety-three cents each. It is accurate for long-distance shooting up to three hundred yards, because its minie ball projectile is imparted with spin as it leaves the barrel. Loading procedure: tear open paper cartridge containing powder and ball with teeth, pour powder down barrel, push bullet with thumb, draw ramrod and push projectile down, pull hammer back, place percussion cap on nib beneath the hammer, aim and shoot.*

He wrote letters home but wasn't at all sure they would arrive at Oakmont. There had been a steady flow of letters from home while he was at Camp Davis, but he knew there had not been enough time for letters to catch up with him in Mississippi. Some of the men admitted to being homesick, and he believed it might also be happening to him. Waiting, being ever on the alert, and not knowing when he would be called into battle was beginning to make him edgy. Almost every day, one or two fistfights erupted, and quarrels developed between men who had been friends for years. Morgan even thought that a good battle with the enemy might help, by diverting everyone's feelings of frustration toward a common enemy.

And a battle did come, brief but deadly. Just before sunup one morning, the rebel camp was startled awake by thundering hooves, spine chilling screams and shouts, and an onslaught of small arms fire. Frantic men grabbed for unloaded muskets that were stacked inside each tent. Many of the sleeping tents were knocked down, and some burned as terrified men scrambled to get out.

Yankee horsemen charged through the mass of confused men who were trying to load weapons, running for their lives, and dying by the enemy's hand. Yankee sabers swung wildly as the Rebels tried to fight back with whatever weapons they could grab. The screams of both men and horses could be heard over the roar of small arms fire. The smell of gun smoke and burning tents quickly filled the air, making breathing difficult.

Morgan picked up a rifle someone had dropped but discovered that it was not loaded. As a rider charged by, Morgan held the weapon by the barrel, used it for a club, and knocked the saber from the man's hand. The Yankee turned his horse, drew his pistol, and fired at Morgan. The shot missed because at that instant Morgan was struck from behind by another horse and knocked out of the path of the pistol ball.

Many of the Tennesseans were killed or wounded before the first shot could be fired in defense. They were outnumbered, probably four or five to one, as the full regiment of Union cavalry raced through the camp back and forth, firing their carbines and pistols and inflicting deadly slashes with their sabers.

Then it was over as quickly as it had started. The Yankee bugler sounded retreat, and they were gone. During the last few minutes of the confusion, a few rebels managed to get off some shots, killing seven of the invaders. One Yankee sergeant was pulled from his horse and captured. When the smoke cleared and the last of the hoof beats were heard, more than 150 men had been severely wounded, and 114 lay dead—most of whom had never fired a shot in anger.

Somebody's darling, somebody's pride, who'll tell his mother where her boy died?

Morgan and the other survivors busied themselves with trying to care for the wounded. Blood was everywhere; in places it gathered in pools or flowed in small red streams. Morgan came upon one blood-soaked soldier who held his hand up to him and attempted to say something. Morgan took a closer look and recognized him as Buddy Green from Mount Pleasant, a young man he had known for several years. He knelt down and held Buddy's hand until the boy died a few minutes later. Morgan found a blanket and placed it over Buddy, who would never return to home and mother.

Morgan had heard many stories of the gore and carnage left by battles, but he had never prepared himself for such gut-rendering devastation as he now witnessed. Someone came along asking if anyone had seen Captain Gentry. Morgan replied that he hadn't seen their commander and volunteered to help look for him. Several others had also joined in the search when someone shouted that he had been found at the edge of camp. Morgan ran to the place where several soldiers were gathering. There, draped across an outgrowth of honeysuckle vines, was the body of Captain Gentry. A saber-wielding Yankee had split his head open like a ripe melon. Morgan was shocked at seeing such a brutal wound.

The overwhelming realization came to him that this was real war, in the full sense of the term, and that his very survival would depend upon his growing accustomed to such wanton brutality. *Oh God,* he thought, *what am I doing here? This is not some glorious adventure, it's a little bit of hell on earth. God, forgive me for my weakness.*

A rush of nausea overcame him, and he had to walk away from the others. When he got to the edge of camp, he continued walking westward along the railroad tracks. He walked a mile or more before turning back, fully aware of the danger of being so far from camp but not really caring. He asked himself several questions, to which he had no answers. Why had the North been so insensitive to the rights of the South? Why had the Southern leaders not tried a little harder to resolve their differences with the North before engaging in something so self-destructive as war? How long would it last? Would he ever get back to Oakmont?

During his absence from camp, two regiments of Confederate infantry under the command of Colonel David Miller had arrived. They were heading south to join the ranks of General Martin Green when one of their mounted scouts came across the now tried but yet unseasoned young Tennesseans. The report from the scout brought Colonel Miller and his men to the bloody site of the one-sided battle. The colonel dispatched ambulances to take the wounded to Jackson and formed a burial detail to dispose of the dead. When the ambulance detail returned from Jackson, they brought orders concerning the survivors of Grierson's raid. The colonel informed the Tennesseans that they were being attached to his unit and ordered them to break camp and form ranks with his men. Shortly after noon Morgan was on the march again, but to where and to what, he didn't know.

Just before sunset they came to a small muddy creek with steep banks. The road crossed the chasm by way of a less than sturdy wooden bridge. Colonel Miller selected a hundred men for picket duty to guard the bridge during the night. At dawn they were to proceed south and join the main party, which would be camping at an old church a few miles farther south.

It happened that Morgan was the only Tennessean selected for the picket duty. He stood by the roadside and watched the other Tennesseans march away to the south while he remained to guard the bridge with total strangers. The sergeant in charge of the pickets would not allow fires to be built, and so the men had to eat whatever cold rations they might have. As total darkness enveloped the camp, a few men engaged in quiet conversations, but most everyone remained silent, listening to the sounds of insects and the lonely call of a night bird. At about ten o'clock they started hearing the distant sounds of cannon and musket fire. The individual reports soon blended together to form a low rumble, much like the sound of thunder when a distant storm begins to form. The sergeant said that he was sure their main unit was under attack. Some of the men wanted to rush to the battle, but the sergeant would not allow it; their orders were to guard the bridge, and those orders would be carried out. After nearly an hour, the cannon fire stopped and the musket firing waned. But random shooting could be heard throughout the night, keeping the men tense and uneasy. There was little rest and almost no sleep for the bone-tired men. Morgan had not had a good night's sleep since he had left Camp Davis.

Morgan could see the first orange hint of sunrise in the eastern sky when they began to hear the approaching sounds of many voices and the rattle of moving vehicles. The sergeant ordered the men to take cover and wait for his orders. The sun was already casting its golden rays on the tree tops when the approaching troops came close enough for Morgan to see the blue coats. The sergeant stood up and yelled, "Men, it's time to scatter! There's no way we can stand up to 'em. If you get away, head south and try to find what's left of our unit. Every man for himself! Now get goin'!"

It was too late. The advancing Yankees had cavalry with them and quickly ran down the fleeing rebels, either capturing or killing most of them. Fate seemed to be with Morgan, and he somehow managed to escape by running into a nearby thicket of heave brush. One Yankee attempted to follow him, but his horse balked and refused to enter the thick undergrowth.

Morgan had crawled under some honeysuckle vines and was only a few feet away as he pondered whether or not to shoot at the man. He realized that if he fired a shot, he would probably be killed by the other cavalrymen, even if he did manage to kill his pursuer. He chose to remain quiet and remembered someone saying, "Discretion is the better part of valor." The rider again tried to force his mount into the entanglement but was almost dislodged from his saddle as the horse reared up on its hind legs. Morgan heard the rider swear and berate the animal as he rode away.

For nearly two hours Morgan heard the familiar sound of a large military unit moving by—the clip-clop of the horses, the crushing of gravel as many wagons and heave gun rolled by, and the never-ending chatter of hundreds of foot soldiers. He remained hidden in the honeysuckle vines until he could hear no sound other than the wind in the leaves. When he was sure there was no danger of being seen, he eased out of his hiding place and started making his way toward the south, staying clear of the roads.

Later, after putting time and miles between himself and the site of the rout, his head still reverberated with the screams of men being killed or wounded by fellow countrymen. Weary and woeful, with no effort to conceal himself from possible danger, he finally sat down at the base of a large water oak, leaned back against the massive trunk, and slept.

When he awoke it was dark and cold. He had slept all day and into the night. He took his blanket from his bedroll, wrapped it around his shoulders, and returned to his position at the base of the oak. He remained there until morning, sometimes sleeping but mostly remembering the events of the last two days, his initiation into the war. He could not shake the memory of that first raid; the blood, the carnage, the smoke, and all the terrible sounds of battle came rushing back to him. He tried to direct his thoughts back to the pleasant times and friendly people at Oakmont, but to no avail. He was simply overwhelmed with the memories of the current events and unable to replace them in his mind.

When morning light finally came, he gathered his scanty possessions and started walking southward again. As he walked he considered his options. He would like to rejoin the Tennesseans that he had been with since Camp Davis, but he knew the chance of finding them was slim. He reasoned that he would find some safety in joining the first Confederate unit he could find, and that happened to be Colonel Francis M. Cockrell's Missourians.

They were camped several hundred feet off a small dirt road and hidden by a grove of scrub oaks. Because Morgan was staying clear of all roads as he made his way, he suddenly came upon their camp without even being challenged. One of the pickets said that he saw Morgan but knew he was a rebel by his dirty gray uniform.

The men were finishing a meager meal of salt beef, cornbread, molasses, and hot coffee when Morgan came upon them. He could not remember when he had last eaten, and so he gladly accepted some of their food when it was offered. At least it would ease his hunger pains.

Later that same day, May 1, 1863, he found himself just west of Port Gibson, fighting side by side with the Missourians along a brushy creek bank. Colonel Cockrell had been ordered to counterattack Grant's advancing forces as a diversionary measure.

Grant, unable to take Vicksburg with a direct assault, had taken his army across the Mississippi River and down the west bank to a point just southwest of Port Gibson. They had again crossed the river and were heading north-northwest along the east bank, in the general direction of Vicksburg. Grant's plan was to attack the well-fortified city from the south, through the swamps. After discovering what Grant was up to, the Southerners threw every obstacle available into his path. All units in the general region, regardless of size, were ordered to resist in whatever way they could. Cockrell had obeyed the orders by attacking a full brigade of over four thousand men with less than eight hundred men.

Not expecting such a courageous move, the Yankees had initially been sent reeling back. Cockrell's men followed them across a small creek and did some damage to Grant's right flank, but soon the enemy brought in fresh troops. The Union began advancing back through thick timber and dense powder smoke toward the Missourians. Morgan witnessed his new comrades falling all around him; their battle line steadily receded as overpowering waves of blue-coated infantry assaulted their front and flanks.

The tide had turned and the skirmish was lost. There was no hope of Southern reinforcements arriving, leaving only one course of action. Cockrell ordered his bugler to sound retreat, and the survivors quickly withdrew back across the creek and into the cover of the deep woods. Brave men swallowed their pride and ran for their lives, some abandoning all possessions.

Again Morgan was forced to run for his life. Again he was separated form a unit that he had not been with long enough to get to know his fellow soldiers. His emotions were mixed as he felt both anxiety and frustration. This was not what he had expected war to be like. He wanted to stay with one group long enough to get to know his comrades. Instead, it seemed as though he was only going around in circles.

In the mass confusion of total rout, Morgan found himself separated from everyone. Then there was Jake, a lanky sharecropper from southern Missouri, who appeared at his side from out of nowhere. After a few more minutes of running, the two were joined by a short, fat boy from St. Louis, named Luther. The trio made their way toward nowhere in particular, but away from the pursuing Yankees.

Sunset found them in a small brush thicket near the edge of an abandoned cotton field. "What do you think we should do now?" Luther asked, directing the question to Morgan. "I don't think I can go any further."

"This is all new to me," Morgan replied, "what do you think, Jake?"

"I'm not sure of anything," Jake answered. "All I know for sure is that I'd like to be back home, with my feet under Mommy's table."

"We can keep heading south and look for what's left of the unit, or we can lie low and hope to make contact another group," Morgan suggested. "Right now, we need to find a place to spend the night."

"I agree with Morgan," Luther said. "Let's find a place to sleep. I've got some two-day-old corn dodgers that I'll share with the two of you; they'll help a little."

"I think the odds are much greater of running into a Yankee patrol than of finding our boys," Morgan said.

Just then Jake got an excited look on his face as he pointed to something across the cotton field. "Look, there's an old building over yonder. See, just to the right of that tall stand of trees."

The building appeared to be an old barn and was barely visible through the trees. It was on the opposite side of the field from where the three crouched in concealment.

Suddenly the last trace of the setting sun was cut off by the leading edge of a rapidly approaching thunderstorm. Little discussion was necessary as they hastily agreed to head for the barn. At first there were only a few sprinkles, but soon the rain began to come down in sheets. Although they were quickly soaked to the skin, they realized that caution was still very necessary. Luther insisted on cutting across the field, but the other two convinced him that it was better to be wet than dead. They heard muffled voices and stopped. The voices soon faded away as the sound of the thunderstorm intensified. They reached the dilapidated barn and, with continued caution, looked inside and out for either friend or foe. When they assured themselves of being temporarily safe, they each filled their canteen from the downpour off the roof. With drinking water replenished, they went inside and climbed up to the hay loft.

Luther withdrew six corn dodgers from his haversack and handed two to each of his companions. They were cold and stale, but the three young warriors wolfed them down like they were Sunday dinner. Caution gave way to fatigue as the needs of overused and undernourished bodies took over. Sleep quickly consumed the three young men, who should have been back home, attending a candy-pulling or a church social.

Morgan had just arrived at Oakmont, riding a fine black stud. Waiting on the steps of the stately old house were John and Mother Newton, and Sissy, the cook. Standing off to one side, so as not to be too intrusive, were Sissy's twins, Caleb and Rufus, with those big, happy grins on their faces. He would visit with John and Martha before consuming one of Sissy's fine meals. He might even take time to go fishing once again with Caleb and Rufus. It was good to be home. He was just stepping down from the saddle when he awoke from a deep sleep with a start. Instead of the warm embrace he expected from Mother Newton, he received a shock back into reality. Instead of being in Tennessee, he found himself in Mississippi, in a moldy hay loft of an old barn near the little village of Port Gibson.

He remained motionless and quiet for several minutes. As he began to relax, memory briefly took him back to the happy times at Oakmont. Three of his favorite people, other than John and Martha, had been Sissy and her two sons. He thought of all the fishing and hunting he and the boys did together when they were young, and of them working together when they were older. It was almost painful to remember the good food Sissy had prepared over the years for every occasion. He especially remembered breakfast with pan-fried ham, eggs, hot biscuits with gravy, and those fantastic jams and jellies. He could almost hear Sissy saying, "Masser Morgan, does ye want anything else? You knows I'll fix it fo' you. Jest tell me."

His thoughts were interrupted by a nearby sound, and he realized that the two boys from Missouri were also awake. It was near dawn, and he could see dim light through the cracks in the barn. "I don't know what woke me," Morgan whispered, "but I think we had better get out of here." Without the slightest hesitation the three young men slipped down from their makeshift beds and out a side door of the barn. A fifty-yard dash through thick, wet weeds brought them to the cover of a wild plum thicket. From there they could survey the immediate area. All seemed quiet; the only sounds were the melodic notes of a nearby mockingbird and the drip-drip-drip of falling droplets of dew. What had awakened all three near the same time? After the brutal fighting they had so recently experienced, any sound that awakened three sleep-deprived men at the same time would be reason for alarm. After several minutes of motionless observation, alarm gradually changed to caution, but still they waited, watched, and listened.

"What woke y'all?" Luther whispered.

"I don't know," Morgan answered, also in a whisper. "I thought I was the only one awake until I heard one of you moving around."

"We'd better stay here till we know what's goin' on," Jake said.

Then the tension eased and a unanimous sigh of relief came from the trio when an elderly Negro man, bent from toil and age, came around the corner of the barn leading an old red mule, the latter looking even more ancient than its leader. The three soldiers exchanged glances, and without a spoken word or visual sign, they crawled from beneath the plum bushes. They crept through tall weeds and into the nearby woods. In single file they began to slowly make their way southward, through a tangled maze of thick brush and vines. As they drudged along hour following hour, Morgan's thoughts drifted back to Oakmont and the series of events that led to his being in such a perplexing situation.

"I've got to stop and rest for a while," Luther spoke up, and Morgan's thoughts came rushing back from Oakmont to the war. He and his two new cohorts had been plodding along for hours fighting briars, vines, and thick brush, and the suggested rest was welcomed by all three. After a thirty-minute break, they resumed their trek.

Talk was almost nonexistent, except for an occasional "Ah, heck," or something stronger, whenever one of them tripped over a hidden log or a thorn penetrated their clothes. Morgan was learning to lessen some of the unpleasantness of the war with an occasional mental trip back home.

By the time he was eleven, he had taken it upon himself to work with the Negroes in caring for the Oakmont horses, especially the saddle horses. The only animal he had ever ridden, prior to coming to Oakmont, was the family plow mule back in Lewis County, but with diligent instruction from John Newton, he had became a skilled horseman at a young age. How he had loved to work with the horses. *I sure would like to have one of them under me now,* he thought.

As long shadows began to denote late afternoon, they came to a large stand of pine trees where very little undergrowth existed. They decided to stop and rest before leaving the low brush that had been both their cover and their aggravation all day.

They threw their haversacks and bedrolls on the ground, leaned their muskets against a large pine tree, and made themselves as comfortable as possible. After a few minutes of rest, Luther announced, "I'm so doggone hungry I could eat the south end of a northbound mule." Morgan thought to himself that Luther hadn't missed many meals, but he didn't say anything; he sure hadn't known his chubby friend long enough to joke about his weight. Then he remembered having a piece of hardtack. He had noticed the paper-wrapped wafer earlier in the day while looking through his haversack for any extra cartridges. Just as he broke the hardtack into three pieces, they heard the nearby whinny of horses. Slightly startled, they ducked a little lower in the brush.

"Look over there! They're Yanks!" Luther announced in an excited tone that was somewhere between a whisper and a shrill shout.

The other two men positioned themselves for a better look at what Luther had seen. "You're right," whispered Jake. "Sure hope they've got better food than this wormy hardtack Morgan just gave me." Morgan grinned at the humor in the remark; he was really beginning to like this red-faced farm boy.

After watching for a few minutes, Jake started counting the horsemen, who appeared to be gathered around a cooking fire. "One, two, three—heck, they's at least a dozen of 'em."

"They're not going to see us over here," whispered Morgan, "so why don't we just stay put until they leave? They've most likely stopped to cook some hot food. Maybe they'll move on soon."

"I sure don't like being this close to a bunch of Yankees," said Luther. "It gives me the creeps."

"Morgan, I think you're right," Jake offered. "They'll see us for sure if we start moving around."

"Why don't we get some more rest while we wait them out," Morgan said. "They'll surely be gone soon." The others agreed with him and went about making themselves comfortable for the wait.

Morgan had made a big miscalculation. No more than thirty minutes had passed when he observed more mounted troops arriving to join the others. A short time later, foot soldiers arrived by tens, twenties, and hundreds. Among the later arrivals were many horse-drawn wagons and cannons. By nightfall, hundreds of small tents had been erected, and dozens of cooking fires illuminated the area. To Morgan's relief, none of the tents were closer than three hundred yards from where they were hiding. The Yankee camp had grown toward the south, away from where he and his comrades had first spotted the few horsemen.

Morgan began to realize the significance of what they were observing. Their hiding place was only a stone's throw from the bivouac of one of Grant's main Union forces, but they were out of options. They could only remain hidden, quiet, and hungry. A gentle breeze came up from the south, which put the three rebels directly in position to smell the camp cooking. Routine sounds of encampment drifted their way: an occasional boisterous laugh, the clanging of cook pots, a call for someone to report to his commanding officer, quick steps, and the ever-present neighing and snorting of horses. Morgan finally surrendered to sleep, but he did not dream he was back at Oakmont, partaking of one of Sissy's famous meals.

He awoke to the pressure of a hand on his shoulder. A very low "Shh," came from the person who had awakened him. "Want some food?" It was Jake. "They all went to sleep, even the guards, except the out pickets. I foraged us some of their victuals. Ain't much, but it'll drive away the hungers." He directed the remarks to both Morgan and Luther, who was now awake. Jake produced a gallon-sized porcelain cook pot and a bundle of something wrapped in coarse cloth. "I got us some stew, three slabs of skillet bread, and enough molasses cookies to last a week."

Slivers of moonlight found its way through the pine boughs as the three young rebels sat there in the cool of the early morning, consuming a hearty portion of the enemy's food. Although cold and not very well-seasoned, it was most satisfying to the three boys. When they had eaten their fill, Jake told them how he had been too hungry to sleep, and how he had decided to look for something to eat. "One Yank walked right by me while I was taking the bread and cookies out of a big wooden box in the back of a wagon. Most of the fires had burned out, and it was kinda dark. He said howdy, and I said howdy, and he just walked on by. Thought I'd been caught for shore. But I reckon he saved both our lives by going on to his tent, 'cause I'da killed him, and they'da killed me."

Jake pulled another molasses cookie from the cloth wrapper and ate it before continuing. "They got pickets in every direction, even behind us. Most of 'em are sleepin', but we'd better not try to move now."

"I think they'll move out as soon as daylight comes," Morgan said. "If we can just stay here, without being discovered, we'll be a lot safer than trying to move out."

"We've stayed this long, might as well stick it out a little longer," threw in the fat boy from St. Louis.

"I agree," said Jake. "The sun will be up in a few hours, and they'll be gone. I got a full belly, and now I'm gonna get some sleep."

"One of us had better stay awake, in case one of the pickets should come our way," Morgan said to Luther as Jake started quietly snoring. I'll take the first watch and wake you in a couple of hours. Jake has done his part tonight."

Chapter 5

To pass the time during the first watch, Morgan let his thoughts go back to Lewis County, Tennessee, to the day of his mother's funeral—and the day he first met John and Martha Newton. December 2, 1853, had been a very cold day. He remembered the little swirls of snow that danced around as gusts of frigid air whisked across the old churchyard. Heavy, dark clouds had threatened to bring more than the occasional flurries that had been sporadically occurring during the morning.

Sounds of sobbing, at times almost inaudible, came from some of the women among the small group of friends and neighbors who had assembled around an open grave. A white-haired old preacher, a circuit rider from nearby Hohenwald, spoke encouraging words about meeting again someday in the hereafter. Then a church deacon gave a long prayer for the soul of the departed one, and for the young son she was leaving behind. When the amens were said, the black-frocked old preacher led the group in singing "Amazing Grace" and "Blest Be the Tie." His mother was then lowered into her final resting place in the cemetery behind the old Baptist church, the place where she had worshiped since first coming to the area as a new bride eleven years earlier. After three years of grieving for the husband, who had preceded her in death, she now took her place beside him. She would spend eternity beside the only man she had ever loved.

He remembered shivering from the cold, and from the deep sadness in his heart. He was alone. A few days earlier his mother, knowing she was near death, had called him to her bedside. "Morgan, you're going to need a lot of help in the coming years, and I'm afraid I won't be here to help you. I've written a letter to John Newton, one of my relatives, who'll see that you're properly cared for. Son, you'll have things available to you that I could never dream of giving you. Remember what I've told you: always do your very best at whatever you try, and above all, keep your faith in God."

He hadn't really understood the meaning of what his mother said and had, in fact, forgotten her words. But upon seeing her wooden casket lowered into the freshly dug hole, he remembered her words and understood that she had been trying to prepare him for that day. A burst of sadness had overcome his resolve to be brave, and he began to cry softly.

Morgan did not know the well-dressed lady who moved to his side as the dirt was being thrown onto his mother's coffin. She and a man, both strangers to him, had arrived after the services started. Morgan had observed them talking to one of the neighbors who was standing to the rear of the little assembly. The neighbor had said something to the strangers as he pointed toward Morgan.

He remembered how the first scoops of frozen dirt made loud, hollow sounds as they hit the wooden box. He forced himself to watch and was overcome by the realization that he would never see his mother again.

Everyone had stood there—the newly orphaned boy, the strange lady and her gentleman companion, and a score of friends and neighbors—until the grave was completely covered. After the mound was shaped and patted down, the strange lady took the single rose she had been holding throughout the service and placed it on the fresh dirt. She then turned to the boy. "Morgan, I'm Martha Newton," she said in a soft, comforting voice. "Your mother and I were friends, and my husband, John, was her first cousin, so that makes us your kin."

The man, also well-dressed, held out his hand to Morgan, who timidly shook it. "Morgan, I know the last few days have been hard on you, and I'm sure you haven't had time to think much about the future, but Martha and I would like for you to come to our home to live."

He said nothing. After a few seconds he withdrew his hand and shoved it into his coat pocket as he wondered where the lady had found a rose that time of the year.

"It's what your mother wanted for you, Morgan. She said so in a letter she recently wrote to me. She told us all about you, and how she wanted us to take care of you," John continued. "And it's what we want also."

"But this is my home," had answered. "There's a lot of work to do." He tried to make his quivering voice sound older than his nine years. As an afterthought he added, "And I couldn't leave all our stuff. I belong here."

He remembered Martha Newton placing a hand on the his shoulder as she softly spoke. "Morgan, we just can't leave you here alone. We have a home over in Maury County, near Columbia, and there's plenty of room. Please, why don't you just try it? If you don't like living with us, we'll try to make other arrangements for you. But for now, just try it … please?"

At daybreak a bugle sounded, and Morgan awoke from a short but refreshing sleep. Two hours earlier, he had asked Luther to take his turn at guard so he could get a little more sleep. Jake was also awake, and the three young men anxiously watched from their secret hiding place as the Union camp hastily came to life. The cooking fires were restarted by placing new wood on the ash-covered embers.

The Northern boys stood around the fires as they ate breakfast from tin plates and consumed cups of coffee. By sunup the wagon teams were all hitched and the riding horses saddled. Morgan thought that they worked together like a well-oiled machine. Less than an hour after reveille, the last Yankee rode out of sight, heading northeast. The three rebels immediately headed south.

Later in the morning they came to a small, muddy stream. Jake thought the Missourians had crossed it the week before, and he believed they called it Little Bayou Pierre. If he was correct, that would put them somewhere due east of Port Gibson. A few hours later they came to a well-used road that ran in a northeast–southwest direction. Exhausted from trekking through the thick undergrowth in the woods, they decided to stay on the road and continue heading south. They had traveled less than a mile on the road when someone yelled, "Halt and tell us who you are!"

They were happy to learn that they had come upon rebel pickets. The sergeant in charge of the pickets, an older man wearing a tattered uniform, came forward and demanded, "Who are you and what are you doing here?"

Morgan volunteered to speak first. "I'm Morgan Montgomery from Tennessee. We're separated from our unit, and we're trying to find it, or any other outfit we can join up with."

"What about you other two? Speak up," snapped the sergeant.

"I'm Luther Owens, and this here is Jake Richards. We're both from Hannibal, Missouri."

Morgan was glad they had found other rebels, but he was a little uneasy with the gruffness of the sergeant and the looks they were getting from the other pickets.

After the sergeant decided they were truly who they said they were, he sent them to the temporary headquarters of Brigadier General John S. Bowen. When they arrived at the camp, they were first taken to a Captain Berry, who talked to each one of them separately. When it came Morgan's turn to be questioned, Captain Berry said, "I hope you don't take this personal. We've had lots of problems with both Yankee infiltrators and rebel deserters. I want you to tell me every place you've been and every unit you've been with since your induction."

Morgan replied, "Well, sir, I was with a half regiment of Tennesseans, under Captain Gentry. We received word that Grant's army was coming our way, so we were rushed out of Camp Davis, Tennessee, and sent to Jackson, Mississippi. We were never given a unit name, nor ever actually assigned to another outfit. Captain Gentry received orders to take us to Edwards Station to guard the railroad. We were attacked by Grierson's cavalry and lost a lot of our men, including Captain Gentry. Colonel Miller came along and took us into his regiment. We headed south, and on my first night with him, we were attacked by a large Union force. I was separated from everyone. The next day I fell in with Colonel Cockrell and his brigade of Missourians. Two days later we were routed by Grant's army. Jake, Luther, and I got lost from the others, and you are the first Confederates we've come across."

"Young man, it looks like you've had it a little rough for such a short time in the army," said Captain Berry as he smiled. "I'd say you deserve a little rest, but I'm afraid you won't get it today. We're about to go into battle with a brigade and a half against McClernand, who has more than three brigades. Every man is needed. I'll have my sergeant find you boys some hot food. You may rest until you're called on, but be ready."

When Morgan exited the captain's tent, Luther commented, "Well, it looks like we're about to be back in the fighting, but least we're getting to eat something."

"Looks like we'll be fightin' seven days a week till this war is over," said Jake.

*   *   *

Morgan and his two Missouri comrades had just finished a meager meal of corn dodgers, molasses, and fried bacon when word came to take up battle positions. Incoming cannon balls exploded around the waiting Confederates, continuing for several minutes before a wave of blue-coated soldiers came charging toward their lines. Over and over Morgan fired, reloaded, and fired again. Due to a complicated loading procedure, few experienced soldiers could get off more than three shots a minute with the muzzle-loading muskets, and Morgan was not experienced enough to get off more than two shots a minute. The end of the paper cartridge had to be pulled off, and the powder had to be inserted into front of the barrel, followed by a patch and a lead ball. Then a ramrod was pushed the ball down the barrel and tamped it snugly against the powder. The hammer had to be pulled back and a percussion cap placed on a nip, which was located at the rear of the barrel. When the trigger was pulled, the hammer struck the cap, which in turn ignited the powder in the barrel. The exploding powder hurled the ball out the front of the barrel with great force.

So many muskets were firing at one time that Morgan could only hear a continuous roar, and the only way he could tell when his musket had discharged was to feel the kick.

The Union troops were repelled wave after wave, but still they came. Morgan ran out of the paper cartridges and took some from the pouch of a soldier who died only a few feet away. He suddenly felt a tug at his right thigh followed by a sharp burning pain, and he knew he had received his first battle wound. Although the pain was excruciating, he continued to fight.

The grossly outnumbered Confederate troops managed to hold their positions until dark, and the fighting was over for the day. McClernand sent a messenger, under a white flag, asking for an all-night truce while they retrieved their dead and wounded. Bowen agreed to the truce, and both sides went about the business of caring for the wounded and dead. During the early hours of the night, dozens of torch lights could be seen bobbing about in front of the Confederate lines, where hundreds of troops from both sides had fallen during the day. Morgan went to the hastily erected hospital tent for treatment of his thigh, but after seeing hundreds of men with wounds much worse than his, he decided to bandage it himself with a piece of his only clean shirt from his haversack.

CHAPTER 6

Morgan had just finished a hastily eaten meal of cold rations when a sergeant approached and ordered him to join the burial squad. Their job was to pick up the dead and take them to a location behind the lines for later burial. He and another man retrieved one dead soldier who was heavier than usual. It was only when they passed by a large fire that Morgan recognized the body they were carrying. It was Luther, or what was left of him. A cannonball had taken the side of his face away. Morgan felt a wave of deep sadness, and even a little anger, as he helped carry his friend to his final resting place. Luther would never see Missouri again.

By midnight, all the dead they could find with the aid of torches had been moved, and things had settled down all over the temporary camp. The only activity was around the hospital area. Morgan considered going back for treatment but decided that he needed sleep more than a fresh bandage.

The next morning they waited for the fusillade of cannon fire that would signal the forthcoming charge of thousands of screaming Union troops. Nothing came, neither cannon ball nor blue coats. Scouts were sent out to determine just what the enemy was up to. They came back with good news. Sometime during the night, McClernand had pulled his troops back about two miles, and it appeared to the scouts that at least one brigade was missing from McClernand's forces.

General Bowmen sent out word among his men that he had decided to wait and see what McClernand was about. The position they were holding had been well-defended by his men, and there was little reason to move at the present time. He ordered his men to dig more trenches and make ready to wait. The waiting also meant rest which was welcomed by all.

Morgan spent an hour looking for Jake but was unable to find anyone who knew anything about the Missourian. He went back to where he had left his bedroll and other belongings and tried to sleep. His body ached from head to toe. The minie ball that creased his right thigh had left a groove a half inch deep and two inches long. It was beginning to throb with every heartbeat, and he was sure it was becoming infected. Back in Jackson he had seen dozens of rebel soldiers around the makeshift field hospitals who had lost a leg or an arm due to the infection of a small wound. The thought of that happening to him was more disturbing than the fear of being killed outright.

Much of his soreness also came from days of walking and fighting with very little rest, and nights of trying to sleep on the hard, wet ground. He had not slept on a real bed since he had joined the army. There had been army cots while he was in training, but they had not much better than the ground.

Finally his weary body gave in to the much-needed sleep. It was short-lived, however, because a sergeant awakened him two hours later and ordered him to stand picket duty. He could have avoided the duty by reporting his wound, but he decided not to do so. It was hurting less now, and he decided that it wasn't as serious as he had first thought. He had gotten a little sleep, and so he felt duty bound to take his place as picket.

It was well after midnight when another soldier showed up to relieve him from his post. He returned to his bedroll but only slept a couple of fitful hours. An hour before daybreak he was wide awake.

He got up, rolled his blanket and oilcloth bedding, and placed them with his other belongings. Then he dug his tin cup out of his haversack and made his way through the maze of sleeping men, over to the cooking fire that had been kept burning all night. Suspended over the glowing coals was the large, ever-present pot of strong coffee. The bitter-tasting brew actually contained very little coffee but was made instead by adding roasted barley to a small amount of real coffee, the latter being in very short supply. He tilted thee hanging pot and filled his cup. He then seated himself against the base of a nearby oak tree, sipped the foul-tasting brew, and pondered the tribulations of war.

He wondered if the war would ever be over, with all the killing, the wounding, the pain, the great hardships, the deprivation, and the terrible waste of it all. He had seen thousands of men die in the few weeks he had been in Mississippi. He had seen mass graves filled with the broken bodies of men and boys from both sides. Too often the corpses were buried without being identified. He thought about the families of all those unidentified men who would never know what had happened to their loved ones. He had not yet been able to harden his emotions against the onslaught of melancholy that had so burdened him throughout the last few weeks. Some of his battle-seasoned comrades had said it would pass, but it had not yet done so.

Having consumed the cup of make-do coffee, he stood up to go for a refill. Instantly and without warning, his world was engulfed by a blinding flash of orange-white light, followed by silent darkness.

I've got to get up. Promised Mama I'd weed the garden this morning. Lots of work to do since Daddy died. Mama warned me last night that I'd better get out before it gets too hot, and now I've slept too long. It's hotter than an oven already. Got to get up—but I can't. So hot. So much pain. I'll just sleep a little longer.

Morgan drifted in and out of confused perception. On one occasion he felt rough, cold hands force his eyelids open, first one eye and then the other. There was a terrible, unceasing roar in his ears as he faintly heard someone say, "This one won't make it."

Later—minutes, hours, or days; there was no measure of passing time—he became conscious of the smell of sulfur, blood, and decaying flesh. He soon welcomed a return to the solace of nothingness.

Morgan felt anguish with every pulse beat. The realization slowly came to him that he was alive. Then he felt something cool and comforting. Rain! Yes rain. Glorious, welcome rain that cooled his fever-hot skin. Soon his entire body began to feel cooler. He could not open his eyes but knew he was facing the sky because he could feel the water pooling over them, in the inner corners near his nose. He managed to open his mouth slightly, and the droplets moistened his dry, parched lips and trickled down his throat. After a while, his body had cooled to a point that he began to shiver with a chill, and the rain stopped. He soon drifted back into a restless sleep and dreamed that he heard Mother Newton praying for him.

Unmeasured time passed. He awoke and tried to move. But the very attempt caused unbearable pain in his head and upper body, and so for what seemed like hours, he made no attempt to move any part of his body or to even open his eyes. When he finally did look around, he saw stars in the sky and was pleased that it was night. He somehow felt safe in the darkness. As he became more alert, questions came to mind. How long had he been there? What kind of wounds had he received? He knew that he was badly hurt, but he could not move enough to examine himself. More time passed as he drifted in and out of consciousness.

He opened his eyes and saw a fat, white-bearded old man standing over him. The man wore a long, dirty, blood-stained coat that appeared to have once been white. He made all the motions of talking, but Morgan did not hear the words. "I can't hear you," he managed to say. The old man spoke again, with more force, and Morgan strained to understand what he was saying. "We didn't think you would make it. We were ready to give you over to the burial squad. Never thought I'd see those eyes open under their own power." Morgan heard the old man's words, but they were coming to him as an echo from a great distance.

"How bad am I hurt?" Morgan asked, in little more than a whisper, and not sure that the words were actually coming out.

Beside the old man stood a much younger man, also wearing a doctor's coat, but a much cleaner one. "Not nearly as bad as we first thought," answered the younger doctor.

"Yeah, you shoulda been dead days ago," said the old one, almost shouting. "You were picked up two days after the battle. They were fixin' to put your bones in the ground when you made some sign of life. They brought you to us, but I was sure they were wasting their time and ours. Do believe you'll make it now."

"How bad am I hurt?"

"That's enough talk for now. Get some rest and we'll talk later," the old doctor answered loudly.

"I could rest a lot easier if you'd only answer my question."

"I think you have a right to know," shouted the younger one. "You have some fragment damage in your arms and chest, not to mention the older wound to your right thigh that, I might add, was badly infected. The big problem has been from the head trauma caused by the cannon ball exploding near you. But it looks like you're beginning to recover from that. Now, as my colleague has already said, no more talking; you'd better get some rest."

Morgan's sense of hearing gradually returned, but he continued to have pulsating headaches. One doctor told him that he had lost enough blood to kill the average man. He had sustained at least two dozen wounds by fragments from the exploding cannon shell, plus the musket ball wound, but he knew he was much better off than most of the patients around him. Many of them would die, and an equal number would probably be better off dead. Some had body parts missing; others had parts that would never be useful again.

One afternoon, after he had been in the hospital about two weeks, a wagon stopped at the back of his tent. Two large Negro men got down from the wagon and stood just outside the opening at the rear of the tent. At the same time, one of the doctors came into the tent through the front entrance. "Mr. Thomas McLauren, a prominent planter of this area, has invited some of you to partake of his family's hospitality during your convalescences," the doctor announced. "I'm only sending the ones who can be moved without endangering their recovery. These two men"—he gestured toward the two Negroes as he spoke—"will help you to the wagons and drive you out to the plantation." He then motioned the two Negroes to come into the tent. When they were inside he said to the wounded, "There's room for four of you in the next wagon—Stovall, Smith, Grooms, and Montgomery."

Morgan had felt unpleasantly warm all morning, and he was sure the fever was returning. But he wasn't about to tell anyone and maybe spoil his chance of going to stay with the McLaurens, whoever they were. He was elated at the thought of being in a real house again, with real floors and a roof over his head. For weeks the only shelter available to him had been a canvas tent, and even that had not been within reach most of the time.

One of the Negroes picked him up without effort and took him out to the wagon, placing him near the front of the wagon bed beside a man with bandages over his entire head. There was a thick layer of pine straw on the floorboards, which would make the ride a little easier. To Morgan, it was already more comfortable than the hard military cot. When the last of the four had been gently placed in the wagon, the Negroes climbed onto the driver's seat, and the horses began a slow walk toward home. The driver turned to the four passengers, and not knowing whether or not they could hear him, announced, "My name be Moses, an' dis heah's Claude."

Travel was slow. The road had been rutted by thousands of horse-drawn military vehicles and was now almost impassable in places. There were times when the driver had to stop and prompt the horses to back the wagon up, after which he would take to the opposite side of the road. On several occasions he drove off the road and through fields in order to avoid some of the more heavily damaged stretches. Morgan could not see where they were going because of the high sideboards, but he understood the difficulties of the journey from the conversation of the Negroes. The afternoon became hot and dusty, and there was no cover over the wagon. With every bump in the road, one of the passengers groaned or made other noises to indicate pain, another one remained quiet and motionless, and the third one talked endlessly.

As the afternoon progressed, Morgan became sure of what he had suspected before the trip started: his fever had returned. His head hurt worse than it had hurt in several days, and the warm wetness around some of his wounds told him that they were starting to bleed again. He knew that nothing could be done, and he would not burden the Negroes with such information.

He began to feel a little better when the sun went down. The dust disappeared, and the humidity that had made the day so uncomfortable now helped cool the night air. Most of the groaning and talking stopped, and an occasional call of a whip-poor-will could be heard over the rattle of the wagon. Morgan occupied his time by watching the darkened silhouettes of giant trees that extended out over the road, sometimes making the wagon appear to be traveling through a tunnel. When they passed through sections with no trees, he could see bright stars overhead, which reminded him of summer nights back in Maury County. Many a night he had stayed outside until bedtime, talking about unimportant things with his two Negro friends, Caleb and Rufus, or just quietly watching the stars. He wondered if those two were also seeing the stars, and somewhere down the road he fell asleep.

He was awakened by a loud, gruff-sounding voice, which ordered, "Stop that wagon!"

Moses said a gentle "Whoa" to the team, and the wagon came to a stop. As the grogginess of sleep quickly faded, Morgan could hear the abrasive voices of several men and the stomping of many hooves.

"Whatcha got 'n the wagon?"

"We ain't carryin' nuffin' worf nuffin'," one of the Negroes said in fearful reply.

A boisterous voice answered, "Get down from 'at wagon and start walkin'. We gonna see fer ourselves, and we're a taking this wagon. One of youse get up there and see what they hauling."

Morgan heard the clip-clop of a horse's hooves as it walked close to the side of the wagon. The inside of the wagon became dimly illuminated by lantern light, and he could see a man's head behind the lantern. The man leaned over in the saddle for a closer look, and Morgan could see the dirty blue cap, handlebar mustache, and stubble beard. He even smelled the man's putrid breath as he yelled to his companions, "We done caught us some dog-bait rebs. 'Em old niggers was tryin' to slip 'em past us in the dark."

The man with the boisterous voice spoke again. "Throw 'em Rebs out and cut their throats. A couple of ye ride after 'em old niggers; they're running down the road. Ketch 'em and kill 'em for helpin' the Rebs."

Morgan felt himself being roughly dragged from the back of the wagon. He was thrown across one of the other wounded soldiers, who had been pulled out before him. As several men roughly pulled the last of his companions from the wagon, someone stepped in the middle of his chest, and he almost passed out. The man with the bad breath asked, "Somebody got a sharp knife?"

The lantern, which was now being held by one of the mounted horsemen, gave enough illumination for Morgan to see thick underbrush growing along the edge of the road. With every ounce of energy he could muster he made a desperate attempt to get to his feet. *God, I need your help, but your will be done, not mine.* Terrible pain hindered every motion, but the great stimulus called fear gave him one last shot of adrenalin. Somehow he was successful in getting up on one foot and the opposite knee, a stance from which he made a stumbling run toward the bushes. Several shots rang out. Just as he was about to reach the safety of cover, he felt something slam into his back.

Meanwhile, the two Negroes, who were being pursued by a trio of horsemen, had left the road and hidden in the thick brush. The three riders sent to kill them heard the shooting back toward the wagon and gave up the search. After the voices and the clopping of hooves had faded away, Moses and Claude made their way back to the road and began walking toward home. It was after midnight when the two tired but happy-to-be-alive men knocked on the outside kitchen door at the big house.

The cook, Sudie, answered the knock. "Lawdy me, we done thought ye both be dead."

"We almost was," said Moses. "Some Yankee men done stop us on de road and take de wagon. Dey don take de young soldier boys what we was bringin' back wid us."

"Come on in an chunk up da far. I'll go wake Masser Thomas."

CHAPTER 7

Thomas McLauren represented the third generation of McLaurens to work the fertile soil of Honeywood Plantation. Honeywood was among the finest plantations in all of Mississippi, consisting of four thousand acres of excellent farm land. The main house, the McLauren home, was a stately, three-story house with symmetrical facade, evenly-spaced windows, and six large fluted Corinthian columns that extended upward from the porch to the hipped roof. The roof extended out to cover the upper level balcony and the front porch, both of which ran the full width of the house. Each of the fourteen rooms had twelve foot high ceilings.

The beautiful home, in which Thomas lived with his wife, Charlotte, and two children, Charity and Charles, was surrounded by large trees, workers' cabins, and several barns and other farm buildings.

Charity, the eldest of the two children, liked to spend as much time as possible outdoors, making the rounds with her father, riding her favorite horse, or visiting with the Negro women around the plantation as they did their work. By the time she was twelve years old, she could hitch a team of horses to a wagon or buggy and drive as well as any man on the plantation. Charlotte did not approve of Charity's tomboy ways, but Thomas took pride in the fact that she loved plantation life.

Charles, on the other hand, did not like the hot sun, the dust, and the smell of horses. He preferred instead to read a good book in the cool of the veranda. At an early age he decided that he wanted to be a medical doctor. That pleased Charlotte very much; she would give him the education and refinement that she had wanted for Charity. Thomas would have preferred that he learn the ways of running a plantation, but he reluctantly agreed to provide Charles with an education in the field of medicine. When the boy turned thirteen, Thomas made arrangements to send him to an eastern school in preparation for his medical training. Rumors of an impending war grew stronger, and after only two years at school, Thomas asked him to return to Honeywood.

Many of the eligible young gentlemen of central Mississippi were vying for Charity's affections, but no one was able to interest her in more than a platonic friendship. She was an outgoing person with many friends of both genders. Thomas and Charlotte gave several gala balls each year that were attended by people from Jackson to Natchez. Hopeful young men stood in line for the privilege of dancing with the young lady of stunning but unpretentious beauty.

It was said throughout the area that one could count on the McLauren's grand Christmas ball to be the most festive event of the year. It was only a few days before Christmas when Charles arrived home from school. Although the clouds of war hung dark and heavy over Honeywood, Charlotte and Charity made sure that the Christmas celebration of that year, 1860, would surpass all others, in honor of his homecoming.

The slaves of Honeywood had their own festivities during Christmas time. That year, everyone who was not needed at the big house to help with the ball was given two days off. Thomas provided them with a pair of large hogs, plenty of vegetables, and dried fruits for pies. On Christmas Eve the men roasted the hogs all day over open pits of hot embers. While the men gathered around the cooking pits to joke and frolic, the women remained in their cabins, each cooking their favorite dishes to go with the hog meat. There was cracklin' bread, hominy, collard greens, parsnips, cabbage, dried beans, and chick peas, and for dessert, apple pandowdy, and pumpkin pie. Near the end of the day, the cooked pork was divided among all the slaves, to be taken to their quarters and eaten with the food prepared by the women.

After the big meal of the day, which was eaten in late afternoon, all the slaves got together in the big yard in the center of the slave quarters for a juba dance. No one knew where the juba originated; it may have been brought over from Africa, or maybe the slaves invented it after they came to America, out of the need for their own kind of rhythmic release. It was a very active dance, characterized by striking the right shoulder with one hand, the left shoulder with the other, then striking the hands together, then patting the hands on the knees—all while the feet kept time with the music.

A banjo and several homemade musical instruments were brought out and tuned. Soon everyone was either singing or dancing to the music. The inhabitants of the main house fell asleep that night to the mirthful sounds coming from the slave quarters, each looking with anticipation to the next night, when their own Christmas festivity would take place.

All Christmas days started early for the McLaurens and their servants. As was customary, that Christmas day started with everyone up and dressed before daylight. As tradition had it, they started the day with a round of hot custard, followed by an exchange of gifts between family members. Then gifts were passed out to the house servants, which consisted of bags of candy, fresh fruits, and small personal items, such as combs or brushes. After the gifts were admired and thank-yous were said, it was time for everyone to begin work. Furniture had to be moved to make room for the dancing.

These celebrations usually lasted all night, with many guests leaving after breakfast the next morning. Bedrooms had to be prepared for the older guests who needed to rest or sleep before traveling home, and for those who would travel great distances to get there. Charlotte insisted on every piece of furniture being dusted and polished, even if it had been done within the previous few days.

Sudie, the head cook, was assigned six servants to help with kitchen duties. Many of the cakes, pies, and other desserts had been prepared in advance, but mountains of food had to be cooked that day. Beverages by the gallon were mixed, blended, or cooked for the occasion. By late afternoon, with preparations completed, everyone retired to their rooms for a short rest and to dress for the early evening arrival of the guests.

The downstairs rooms of the house were divided by a wide hall that ran from the front gallery to the rear of the house. On each side of the hall were heavy sliding doors of solid mahogany. When the sliding doors were opened, the front parlor, hall, and dining room formed a large suite across the entire front of the house, which accommodated the more than two hundred people who were expected for the event. Tables, sideboards, and buffets were laden with every kind of delicacy one could wish for, and six servants remained on hand to serve food and drink on a continuing basis.

The guest, all wearing their finest clothes, usually started arriving by late afternoon in carriages, buggies, and light wagons. Many of the men, especially the younger ones, arrived on horseback.

There was no scheduled Christmas dinner, per se, due to the large number of guest, but food was temptingly available at any time. Servants were there to assist the diners when they were ready.

Although the temperature was cool, most of the men congregated outside to smoke and to talk of politics, and of a possible war. The ladies made the rounds inside of the house, catching up on the latest fashions, and the latest gossip. Much laughter could be heard over the never-ending conversations, both inside and outside the house. It was a very happy and festive occasion.

At sunset the musicians from Natchez started playing chamber music but later changed to a livelier dance tempo. Soon all available floor space was awhirl with dancers.

At around ten o'clock, a servant came to Thomas and said that a messenger wanted to talk to him at the front door. Thomas went outside to talk to the man. It was several minutes before he returned to the ballroom. He climbed onto a chair and motioned for the musicians to stop playing, which they did immediately. The room became very quiet, and Thomas addressed his guests.

"Ladies and gentlemen, I've just received some important news." He paused and looked around the room to make sure he had everyone's attention. "My friends and neighbors, it's with mixed emotions that I bring you this news. As you all must know by now, Mr. Lincoln has been declared the winner of the November presidential election. I have just received the news that, as the direct result of the election, the state of South Carolina has passed an ordinance of secession from the Union."

He stopped at that point, waiting for the reaction of the crowd. For a moment the room remained quiet, and then someone began to applaud. Someone else followed, and soon almost everyone in the room began clapping their hands and cheering wildly. After the noise subsided, Thomas continued, "The news is personally troubling to me. I fear that war will come as a result of this action, and that we will all be pulled into the conflict." More applause erupted. He was a little surprised that so many people would take that kind of news so lightheartedly.

Realizing that it was not the time to try to impress upon them the seriousness of the arising situation, he gave up and said, "But enough of this negative talk—let's get back to the dancing." He turned toward the band and said, "Gentlemen, music, please."

Thomas had been concerned that such news would put a damper on the festivities, but to the contrary, almost everyone seemed elated, some even ecstatic over what they had been told. The music and the dancing were livelier than ever. Three months and eighteen days from that Christmas night, the Civil War started.

Thomas McLauren and the entire household had been concerned when Moses, Claude, and the Confederate soldiers they had been sent to get failed to return on time. At midnight he sent his family off to bed, telling them that Moses and Claude probably had to wait at the hospital for some reason, maybe for the release of the patients. But in his heart he felt that trouble had befallen the group, either while on their way to the hospital or on their way back with the patients. He hadn't heard of any large units of Yankees being in the area, but recent reports of small marauding bands of enemy cavalry had been numerous. He went to his study while he waited but was unable to focus his mind on the task of reading. He had just decided to take a couple of his men and go looking for the truant party when Sudie knocked at his study door.

When he entered the kitchen, he was pleased to see that Moses and Claude were both unharmed. But his mood quickly changed when they told him what had happened on the road. He sent Claude to have one of the stable hands saddle two horses and hitch a team to one of the light wagons. He and Claude rode on ahead while Moses followed in the wagon. After an hour of riding, they came upon the forms of three men stretched out along the side of the road. Thomas dismounted and walked over with a lantern to get a closer look. He was appalled at what he saw. The blood-covered bodies gave witness to the butchery that had been their end. Each man's throat had been cut from ear to ear. Claude dismounted and came over to look at the grotesque sight. His only verbalization was a low groan when he first saw the men. After a few moments of silence, Thomas spoke. "Didn't you tell me there were four men?"

"Yessuh, dey was one mo," Claude said. "Dem Yankee men must've took 'em."

Thomas held the light a little higher and looked all around before asking, "Are you sure there was another one?"

"Yessuh. Dey was one mo."

Moses, who had just arrived with the wagon, confirmed what Claude had said. "Yessuh, day was sho one mo."

The three of them took up the grim task of loading the dead soldiers. When the last soldier had been placed in the wagon, Thomas said, "Well, let's get back to—listen! Did either of you hear something?"

"Yessuh, I believe I hear sumpin' in dem bushes," Moses said, pointing to the low brush along one side of the road.

"Shh," Thomas hushed. The three men listened intently, but for a moment, the only sound they heard was that made by one of the team horses pawing the ground. Then Moses spoke, "Heah dat? Somebody a groaning—ovah in dem bushes."

Thomas held the lantern high and worked his way into the thick brush where Moses had pointed, followed by the two slaves. Fifty feet from the road they found Morgan's crumpled form, blood-soaked and near death. In short order they were heading back toward Honeywood in a trot, with four Confederate soldiers in the wagon—three dead, and one almost dead.

Charity was awakened about four o'clock in the morning by activity downstairs. She slipped on a robe and slippers and went down to see what was happening. Two lamps in the kitchen burned brightly, and light also came from the small bedroom next to the kitchen. The room had been Sudie's at one time, and she still used it during holidays when she had to spend long hours preparing food. Charity heard busy voices coming from the room and hurriedly crossed the kitchen to see what was going on. When she got to the door, she saw her father and Sudie, one on either side of the small bed, and Claude and Moses watching from nearby. She observed a pan of bloody water on the bedside table, and Sudie appeared to be washing the back of the person on the bed. Her father noticed her standing in the doorway and exclaimed, "Charity, you shouldn't be down here! I'm sorry, but you must go back to your room."

"What is it, Father? What has happened? Who is that?"

Thomas came around the bed, took Charity by the arm, and led her out into the kitchen. "I'm sorry to be curt, but that was not something a young lady should see. I'll tell you all about it in good time, but we have a young soldier in there who's badly hurt. I must get back in there to help Sudie; please go back to your room. I'll tell you and the rest of the family all about it later."

"Very well, Father, but you know I'll not sleep another wink." She climbed the stairs and went to her room. She didn't bother to remove her robe. She thought of lighting the lamp on her reading table but changed her mind. Instead she walked over to one of the large windows and looked out. The sky was clear, and the moon, now approaching the western horizon, still gave off enough light for her to see the surrounding countryside, but her thoughts were on the man on the little bed downstairs.

She had gotten a quick look at him. He had been lying face down, stripped to the waist. Although Sudie had been attempting to wash the blood away, there had still been residue of black, dried blood around what appeared to be a hole in his back, just below his right shoulder blade. Her father had rushed her out before she could see more. She had heard about all the death and destruction caused by the war around the area and across the South, but this was the first man she had seen up close who was a victim of the fighting. She kneeled down by her bed and prayed that the man downstairs would live, and that the dreadful war would soon be over. She then pulled a chair over to the window, and sitting there in the darkness, she was unable to get her mind off the young soldier that her father and Sudie were trying to save. In deep contemplation, she thought about the reports of thousands of other young men who had already been killed or mutilated, and the many thousands who were yet to meet their fate. She pondered the future of her family and Honeywood.

She loved her home and could never envision living any other place. But what would the terrible war bring into her life, with the fighting going on all around her, and now even a wounded soldier in her home? Would she ever again know the peace and tranquility of the plantation life that she had known for over seventeen years? Would all of her family survive the conflict?

For many weeks she had been frightened over sporadic reports of farms and plantations being totally destroyed by the Yankee raiders. There had been one report of a planter being killed over near the little community of Bovina; Union soldiers had hanged him from a tree in his own front yard, after which they burned the buildings and took all the slaves away to serve the Union army. She feared for the safety of all her family, but especially that of her father. He was a Christian and a very prudent man, but she knew he would resist, with force if need be, any attempt to harm anyone or anything on his property.

She had the fortune of having been brought up in a good Christian home, and she had developed a strong faith at an early age. There might be hard times ahead, but she believed God would take care of her needs, and she knew that faith could be a major factor in her survival. She remembered a Bible verse to which her mother so often referred, 1 Peter 3:13: *And who is he that will harm you if ye be followers of that which is good?*

Charity took it upon herself to help care for the wounded soldier who was lying unconscious in Sudie's old room. In the days and weeks that followed, she spent much of her time sitting with him. She would spend hours just watching him breathe and wiping his brow with a cool, damp cloth. At first his breathing had been shallow, and there had been much talk among the servants that he was going to die. Charity would promptly scold them when she heard such talk. She would say long prayers for the young man and felt that they were being answered when his fever dropped some and his breathing became a little stronger.

She thought he was the most handsome man she had ever seen. But all she knew about him was his last name. The papers on the four wounded soldiers had been lost the night the Yankees stopped the wagon on the way from the military hospital. Moses remembered that he had been called Montgomery.

"Missie Charity, fer weeks ye been spendin' all yo time wit that soldier boy, takin' care of 'im like he was kin. Whatcha gonna do if he dies?"

"He's not going to die, Sudie. I've been praying for him every night, and I know the angels are watching over him. He'll wake up soon, you just wait and see. Oh, he's so handsome. I can't wait to talk with him."

"Child, you talk like ye be in love wit dat boy. What's Miz Charlotte an Masser Thomas gonna say 'bout you carryin' on over some boy ye don eben know? Ye knows da not gonna let ye be hanging round no po' white trash."

"Oh Sudie, don't say such a thing. He's not trash. I can just tell by his looks that he's from a quality family. Look at those beautiful white teeth, that smooth skin, and that masculine physique."

"Hush yo mouf, child! Shame on ye for talkin' like dat!"

"Sudie, all that means is that he has a nice body."

"I doen care, still ain't polite fo' no proper young white lady to talk 'bout a man's body. Lord, what is ye gonna say next?"

"Sudie, I love you, but you're such an old fuddy-duddy. I am a very proper young lady, but I'm going to nurse this boy back to good health. And anyway, I know you like him too. You, Claude, and Moses have been taking turns around the clock taking care of him."

"Missie Charity, as long as ye jes sits wit 'im, feeds 'im, wipes his face wit dat damp cloth, an holds his hand, I reckon itta be all right wit me. Jes mind ye, me an Moses and Claude still be doin' the washin' and changin', or whatevah he need."

"Well, good mornin' to ye. Ye sho been sleepin' a long time," came the voice from somewhere close to Morgan. "For a while we didn't know fo sho if ye be dead or alive." A nurturing hand was placed under the back of his neck, raising his head slightly. "Heah, ya needs to drink some ah dis heah water." A glass of cool water was held to his lips, and he took a sip. "Dat's good, now take a little bit mo' fer me," the gentle voice urged. He took another small sip, and the hand eased his head back to the pillow. He drifted back into a feverish slumber.

Some time later he heard, or dreamed that he heard, a young, soothing voice that said, "Handsome soldier boy, please get better." A caring hand wiped his face with a cool, damp cloth. He continued to feel the presence of someone nearby, but he could not muster the strength to speak or even to look around the room.

*　　　*　　　*

Time passed. The room was pleasantly dark when Morgan awoke to subtle busy sounds that at first he could not identify. Then something inside him stirred as he smelled the faint aroma of frying bacon, and he recognized the pleasant sounds of an early morning kitchen. In his foggy state of mind, the notion came to him that the sounds were being made by his mother as she cooked his breakfast. Absorbed in such agreeable thoughts, he almost expected her to enter the room to tell him that it was time to get out of bed and get ready for school. He reasoned that if she did, he would just tell her that he didn't feel like going to school this morning. He ached from head to toe and was sure he had fever. She would put her hand on his forehead and know he was telling the truth. He attempted to raise himself to a sitting position but did not have the strength to do so. The effort caused a burst of excruciating pain in his head and throughout his body. He relaxed, and the pain slowly subsided to a more bearable level. He listened and smelled as nostalgic stimulation replaced much of the pain.

Yellow rays of light slowly replaced the darkness in the room. He opened his eyes. Nothing he could see was familiar to him—it wasn't his room. He managed the strength to turn his head just enough to look at the wall. He surely didn't know the Negro people in the old tin-plate picture hanging there. Then something back in his subconscious jogged his memory, and he was painfully reminded that his mother hadn't cooked breakfast for him in years. He was overcome by a wave of sadness and befuddlement as he remembered his mother's funeral on that cold and snowy December day, ten years earlier. Everything was twisted and tangled and irrational, and time seemed to have stopped, or even backed up. He was totally confused as he drifted back into a deep, feverish sleep, and the reoccurring dream of Mother Newton praying for him returned. He slept and time passed.

When he next awakened, there was a hint of darkness in the room. Unsure of whether it was early morning or late afternoon, he lay there, trying to recall the events that led to his being in that bed. Like Poe's opium sleep, it was difficult to distinguish between the many dreams and reality. There was a garbled recollection of battles and the hazy hodgepodge of scrambled dreams that had troubled him throughout this seemingly endless voyage through time. Trying to fit the bits and pieces of his random recollection into some sort of orderly thought pattern was extremely vexing. After a short while he became fatigued, and sleep replaced his troubled thoughts.

Hours later darkness had filled the room. Morgan had been awake for what seemed like an hour, savoring the cool quietness, when a nearby voice broke the silence. "Masser, I believes ye gonna make it."

Morgan managed to raise his head enough to see the large bulk of a man standing in the doorway across the room from the bed. The speaker disappeared for a moment and then returned with an oil lamp. Morgan thought he recognized him as one of the Negro men who had come for him at the hospital. He gave Morgan a warm smile and said, "Howdy. They calls me Ole Claude. We sho didn't know for a while if ye was gonna make it."

Morgan instantly liked the old man, who looked strong enough to grab an ox by the tail and sling it over his shoulder. He managed a weak grin and in slightly more than a whisper replied, "Hello, I'm Morgan Montgomery."

"Say, does ye want sompin' to eat? Sudie got some good chicken stew made up." Without waiting for Morgan's answer, he walked to the door and called out, "Hey, Sudie, he awake. I 'spect he be about ready far some of yo stew." Then he turned to Morgan and said, "We been gettin' some thin soup down ye for days, but I don't s'pose you 'member dat."

"I'm afraid I don't," replied Morgan.

A smallish and slightly bent Negro woman came into the room. She carried a wooden tray and placed on the bed beside Morgan. On the tray was a bowl of chicken stew, a slice of freshly baked bread, and a cup of hot tea. "Dis heah's Sudie. She de main cook for Masser McLauren. Sudie and me and Moses been takin' care of ye fo' about two or three weeks. Missie Charity be down heah wit ye a lot too. Sudie, his name Masser Morgan."

"Ole man, ye sho do talk a lot," Sudie said to Claude as she gave him a big smile. She broke the bread into small pieces, crumbled them into the thin stew, and spoon-fed the mixture to Morgan. She gave him sips of hot tea between bites. When about half the food had been eaten, he said that he could eat no more and thanked her. "Ye needs to eat more'n dat, but I be bringin' more far ye later," she said and left the room. Claude excused himself and followed Sudie out. Morgan soon returned to the land of slumber.

CHAPTER 8

Morgan opened his eyes to see a well-dressed man standing at his bedside. When the man saw that Morgan was aware of his presence, he held out his hand and said, "Hello, young man, I'm Thomas McLauren."

"Hello, sir. My name is Morgan Montgomery," the young man weakly responded.

"You've given us quite a scare. We weren't at all sure you would survive your wounds—that is, all of us but Charity, my daughter. She has been most persistent in her notion that you would fully recover, and I am most pleased that she was right. Now, let me take this occasion to officially welcome you into our home. Please consider it your home as long as you need it."

"Thank you, sir. I'm not sure of how I came to be here, but I do appreciate your gracious hospitality."

"We'll talk about your coming here at a later time, when you are stronger."

"Can you tell me how the war is going? Is there still fighting in this region?"

"Vicksburg is now under full siege, and most of the fighting is being done around that area. We occasionally have stragglers come this way, such as the ones who jumped your party that night. But fortunately for us, most of them only want to pilfer food. We usually get by with the loss of a pig or a few chickens."

Morgan was relieved to know that he was no longer in immediate danger, at least for the present time.

"You're looking a little tired now, so I'll leave you to rest. This room is next door to the main kitchen. You were in such a weak condition when we brought you here, I thought it best to keep you down here where someone would always be present to keep a watchful eye on you. I don't think that is necessary any longer, and so later today I'll have the servants move you to an upstairs bedroom. It will be much quieter there, and you can rest better."

Thomas started to leave, but turned at the doorway and said, "Oh, before I forget, you had a visitor recently. General Forrest came by a few days ago; said he was camped a few miles away and dropped by to check on you. He ended up staying the night with us, and we had a very pleasant conversation. He talked a lot about a place called Oakwood and the people who live there, and he mentioned that he first met you there. He said to tell you that he would be back later."

"Did he say how he found me?" Morgan asked.

"I don't remember for sure, but it was something about one of his scouts reporting that a wounded soldier named Montgomery was here," Thomas answered. "He also said something about sending others to check it out, but I can't recall the details. There are always Confederate riders stopping in for food for themselves and their animals, so it could have been any one of them."

Morgan really didn't want to be moved to another room, but he could not bring himself to tell his host that he liked hearing all the sounds associated with the cooking activities, and that he liked having Sudie and the others pop in so often. He would miss that but didn't want to appear to be ungrateful. That afternoon Moses came with two younger Negro men that Morgan had not seen before. One of the younger Negroes effortlessly picked him up and carried him up the winding stairs, down the wide hall, and into an elegantly furnished bedroom.

The spacious new room was well lit by six high windows, three on either side of double French doors that opened onto a small balcony. Moses had the drapery pulled back and tied so that, from the large canopy bed, Morgan would have a grand view of the portion of the plantation that lay behind the house. Morgan was then pleased with the move; he could see the circle of about thirty small, whitewashed slave cabins. Past the slave quarters stood two large barns, around which were clustered several smaller barns, shops, and animal pens. Beyond that he could see sprawling fields with neat green rows a mile long. Tired from the move, he only enjoyed the view for a few minutes before falling asleep.

He awoke two hours later. Someone had opened the windows, and the room was pleasantly cool. He could hear the sounds of routine plantation life, which brought pleasant memories of Oakmont. He could hear sounds of wood being chopped, which was a never-ending chore on any plantation. Some dogs were barking at whatever there was to bark at in the late afternoon, and in the distance several men were singing the kind of rhythmical work song that he had so often heard while growing up at Oakmont. Somewhere nearby he could hear the happy, shrill voices of children at play.

He heard a slight sound and turned to see a boy, who appeared to be fourteen or fifteen years old, coming through the door. The boy was slim and somewhat frail, and he looked as though he had spent little time exposed to the sun or other outside elements. "Hello! Hope I'm not disturbing you," the boy said.

"Not at all," Morgan assured him.

"My name's Charles McLauren."

"Hello, I'm Morgan Montgomery."

"Yeah, I know. I've dropped in on you several times before, while you were in the room downstairs. And I've heard my father and sister talk about you a lot, especially my sister."

"I've met your father, but I haven't had the pleasure of meeting your sister."

"Well, she's acting a little strange lately. She spent most of her time helping Sudie and the men take care of you while you were unconscious. Now that you're awake, she's started acting shy, and that girl has never been shy in her life. I don't understand it at all."

"Well, I'd like to meet your sister. What is her name?"

"Charity. I'm sure she will be around soon. But for now, is there anything that you need? Is there anything I can have the servants bring you?"

"No, thank you. I've been well cared for. I suppose the only thing I really need is time."

"I'll leave you alone, then. There's a hand bell on the table by your bed. If you should want anything, just ring it good and loud." Charles went out and eased the door shut behind him. Morgan was content to just lie there and listen to the familiar farm sounds, basking in the pleasant memories of Oakmont.

It was nearing nightfall when Thomas McLauren knocked gently on the door and came into the room. Following him was an older gentleman carrying a small black doctor's bag. "Morgan, this is Doctor Crawford. He's been dropping in to check on you every few days."

"Hello, Morgan," the doctor said. "It's very good to see you awake."

"Hello, Doctor. I'm afraid I don't remember your previous visits, but I'm sure that I owe my life to you."

"Well, God and I did our part, but you wouldn't be here today had it not been for this family's compassion. I don't think I've ever seen anyone get better care than you've had."

Morgan looked toward Thomas. "I'm sure I can never repay anyone for all that's been done for me."

"Your getting well again will be all the repayment I'll ever want," Thomas assured him.

Doctor Crawford placed his hand behind Morgan's back and pulled him up to a sitting position. "Hold him in that position," he said to Thomas, "while I examine this back wound." The old doctor first removed the bandage, after which he thumped and pressed on Morgan's upper back, causing a rush of pain. "It's lookin' much better," he said, more to himself than to his patient. He then told Thomas to ease him back down, after which he examined Morgan's other wounds. "Young man, you must have an iron constitution. You had a lead ball lodged between two ribs, near your spinal column. You had lost too much blood for surgery, but I felt that I had to remove it to save your life. It's healing very nicely now, and the other wounds also. I'm going to leave the bandages off. You'll be ready to start getting out of bed in another week or two—with help, of course."

Doctor Crawford then directed his comments to Thomas. "If I'm not back in a week, I want you to start having someone help him out of bed and into a chair, once a day, for only a few minutes at first. Then increase it to two times and for longer periods each day. When he's regained enough strength, have him walk a little and stay out of bed as much as he can tolerate."

Shortly after Thomas and Doctor Crawford had left the room, Sudie came in with a large tray of food. "It sho is pleasin' to hear bout you is doin' so good. I heah Doctah Crawford say to Masser Thomas dat you gonna be good as new."

"Well, thank you, Sudie. From what I've been told, I'll have to give you much of the credit. But I think you're trying to kill me now, with all this food. You've brought enough for a field hand."

"Yessah, and I wants ye to eat every bite of it, so's you gets strong again."

Morgan was later awakened by a young Negro boy bringing hot water, soap, a wash cloth, a towel, and a fresh bed shirt into the room. The boy helped Morgan sit upright while he gave himself a pan bath. The Negro then helped him get into the clean shirt and back under the sheet. Soon another servant brought in breakfast, which Morgan ate with vigor. He felt good.

About midmorning there was a gentle knock at the door, and Morgan said, "Come in." Thomas McLauren entered the room, accompanied by two women. "Morgan Montgomery, may I present my wife, Charlotte," he said as he approached Morgan's bed. Charlotte, though very pale, had a delicate beauty that made her look much younger then Thomas.

"Hello, Missus McLauren. Pleased to meet you," Morgan said.

"Well, good morning to you, young man. It's a pleasure to meet you, and an honor to have you in our home," Charlotte replied in a refined Southern drawl. "May I present our daughter, Charity."

Charity looked to be about five and a half feet tall with light brown hair that appeared to be a little sun-bleached at the ends. Her face was slightly tanned, and her beautiful smile was accented by her even, white teeth. Morgan couldn't see the color of her eyes, but they were dark and smiling.

Words failed Morgan. He very much wanted to say something that would impress the lovely creature standing before him, but he only managed to get the words out, "Hello, Miss Charity."

Charity seemed to sense his frustration and came to his rescue by quickly replying, "Hello, Mister Montgomery. What my mother said about the honor of having you in our home goes for all of us. And I'm expecting you to tell me all about yourself as soon as you're a little stronger."

"I'm sure that won't be long, my dear, but for now let us leave him to his rest," Thomas said to his daughter. "There'll be time for talking later." To Morgan he said, "Don't hesitate to let us know of anything you need." With that he turned and escorted the two women out of the room.

Morgan was actually glad that they had gone away so quickly, but he was a little aggravated at himself for becoming speechless when introduced to Charity. She must think him some kind of fool. He had always been suave and witty around the young ladies back home, but now when he really wanted to make a good impression on Charity, he had thought of nothing to say. She was truly beautiful, and he was sure that she was the most stunning girl he had ever met. But he had seen more than beauty. She had an overall wholesome appearance, and unlike most well-bred Southern ladies who went to great extremes to stay out of the sun, the tanned face and sun-bleached streaks in her hair left no doubt that she had spent a great deal of time outdoors.

Morgan soon fell asleep but awoke an hour later with Charity on his mind. He tried to remember every detail about her face. She had full, well-shaped lips, and her teeth were pearly white. He thought her eyes were brown—or were they hazel? The low light had not allowed him to tell the color. Her nose was small and ever so slightly turned up at the tip. She was so beautiful. And her body ... a wave of embarrassment came over him when he visualized her well-formed figure.

*　　　*　　　*

Morgan's wounds were healing nicely. As his strength returned, he started taking walks around the house. First he made his way around the bedroom and then down the spacious hallway and back. The first time he left his room, he discovered freshly cut flowers in an ornamental vase had been placed on a table near his door. Each day there were new flowers there. He wondered if they had been placed there for him, and if so, who had placed them there.

Soon, with help from Moses, Claude, or one of the other servants, he was walking down the stairs to visit with the McLauren family. He began taking his meals with them, and best of all, he started spending an hour or two each day with Charity, relaxing on the big front porch and often carrying on long conversations about frivolous things.

During some of the pleasant times with her, he would forget about the war. The very joy of her presence carried him into a magical world of ecstasy, a world million miles away from the fighting, and he knew that he was falling helplessly in love with this wonderful, beautiful, and virtuous girl. He thought of telling her of his overflowing love, but he could not bring himself to do so because of his fear that she might think him a fool. When he was away from her, his mind was capable of more rational thoughts, and he realized that he would soon have to return to the war. To tell her of his feelings would be taking liberties with her emotions, and that would be neither proper nor appropriate. That was why he always tried to keep their conversations on unimportant things.

One morning they walked about two miles down a long lane, past fields of cotton and corn to a large, spring-fed lake, where they watched two wild ducks playing hide-and-seek in the tall reeds on the opposite side of the lake. They watched for several minutes before beginning their return walk back toward home. As they neared the big house, Charity apparently realized that Morgan had walked farther than usual, and she suggested that they stop for a rest in a rose-covered gazebo. She told Morgan that this was her own private place, a place where she always came when she needed to be alone to think things out if she had something special on her mind. No one else ever came here, but the servants always kept the rose vines neatly trimmed for her enjoyment.

During the walk she had done most of the talking, mostly about her life on the plantation. "Well, is there anything else you want to know?" she laughingly asked.

"Yes. Why Honeywood?"

"What do you mean?"

"I mean, why is this property called Honeywood? You must admit, it's a strange name for a plantation, even by Mississippi standards."

"I'll be glad to answer that question, but first you must agree to be a gentleman and not make any more disparaging remarks about Mississippi standards."

Morgan gave a shy grin. "I'm sorry. I promise not to say anything that would cast disparagement on the great state of Mississippi."

"Morgan Montgomery, you are incorrigible," she replied, trying to sound angry. "Now, if you will just act like a gentleman from Tennessee should, I'll answer your question. When Great-Grandfather McLauren came here to take possession of this land, he camped in a stand of trees by a small stream, near where the house now stands. You know—the stream that furnishes water for the lake behind the barns. A storm came up during the night, splitting an old oak tree from top to bottom. The next morning he discovered that the tree was full of honey, which the servants promptly gathered. While enjoying a breakfast of fresh honey and biscuits, he decided on the name for his new land, thus the name Honeywood Plantation."

At that time the noon dinner bell sounded. Charity took Morgan's hand in hers as she stood up. "My, where has all the morning gone? I'm afraid I've worn you out, with the walking and all my talking. I must apologize," she said, still holding his hand in hers.

"If an apology is due, it should come from me," Morgan replied, "occupying so much of your time lately."

"I'll make a bargain with you," she said, giving him one of her most pleasant smiles. "Let's neither apologize. Let's just enjoy our time together."

Morgan's heart skipped wildly at her words. "It's a deal," he answered. He started to tell her that he had just spent the happiest morning of his life, but he decided against such a remark. "Now, let's go get some food. I'm starving."

They were almost to the house when she slowly released his hand. As he entered the dining room with Charity, he knew beyond a doubt that he was deeply and hopelessly in love with this wonderful Mississippi girl.

During the time Morgan had been at Honeywood, Thomas had taken in several other wounded soldiers, as well as two families from Jackson whose homes had been burned by the Yankees. Almost daily, strangers were taken into the McLauren home; often they were people who had lost their homes in the fighting and needed a meal and a bed for the night. Every chair around the long table was always filled at each meal, and Thomas would make sure that each one left the table with a full stomach. He always tried to keep the conversation off the war, but that proved to be an impossible task. The main topic of every conversation was Grant's siege of Vicksburg.

During one of the noon meals, a man who was fleeing Vicksburg with his family addressed Thomas, "Mister McLauren, I thank you, and I thank God for this food. It's the first respectable meal I, my wife, and two grandchildren have had in weeks."

"Mister Wilson, I too thank God for allowing me to have food to share with those who need it," Thomas said in reply. "Is there no food at all to be had in Vicksburg?"

"None. In the beginning everybody, both rich and poor, had plenty to eat. When the soldiers first came, they brought their own food with them, such as it was. After a while their food ran out, and we all shared with them. Then everything started running short, and soon there was little or no food to be found. Mule meat sold for a dollar a pound, to the folks that had a dollar—that was three or four times what good beef brought before the war. Some of those who had enough money to buy it said it wasn't so bad. But even that ran out. A man who ain't never been hungry can't imagine what it's like, day after day."

"Well. Mister Wilson," Tomas said, "I want you and yours to be well fed when you leave. Where are you going from here?"

"My brother has a farm down near the coast, and he'll take us in till the war is over. It'll take us two or three days to get there, but we'll make it just fine, now that we've had good food and a little rest."

"I'll make sure you take enough food with you for the rest of the trip," Thomas replied.

Almost every day someone would ride by with new reports, most of which looked bad for the Southern defenders. It was the general consensus that Vicksburg would soon fall to the Yankees; the only question was when.

With each passing day, Morgan grew physically stronger and his wounds continued to heal. He had even volunteered to help with some of the lighter chores around the barns. His favorite chore was feeding the horses. He missed the horses back at Oakmont and remembered his own horse, Raven. Morgan had first named him Chesterfield and was going to call him Chester for short. After being curried and brushed, the animal's glossy black coat would shine like a raven in the sun, and so his name was changed. John and Martha Newton had given him Raven as a colt, on his fifteenth birthday. How he had grown to love that horse; he missed him very much, almost as much as he missed John and Martha. He sometimes allowed himself to wonder if he would ever see any of them again.

Each day Morgan's love for Charity grew stronger, but each day he realized that his time at Honeywood was growing shorter. He looked forward to their daily walks with great anticipation. With so many people coming and going at Honeywood, the walks were now his only time to be alone with her. They were past the stage of being shy about holding hands as they walked. Everyone on the plantation, even the servants, knew about their shared emotions, but still the two had not talked about it.

The fighting became so concentrated around the Vicksburg area that there were almost no reports of Yankee sightings around Honeywood. Morgan's strength had improved to the point that he was able to saddle one of McLauren's fine horses and ride around the farm lanes. One morning Charity informed him that she would like to ride with him, and he was exuberant. That afternoon he saddled two horses, and they took a long, slow ride around the plantation. After three hours of riding, they came to a small, clear stream in the middle of a tall stand of pine. Morgan decided to let the horses take water and rest a few minutes. He didn't want to admit it to Charity, but due to the fact that he hadn't spent this much time in the saddle in months, he needed to rest his bones. He dismounted and walked around to the left side of Charity's horse to help her down. As she stepped from the sidesaddle, he placed his hands on either side of her small waist. It was then that he realized he had overestimated his recovery. He momentarily lost his balance and had to take a small step backward to regain it. Charity, not expecting the movement, sensed that she was about to fall and threw her arms around Morgan's neck. He felt her firm body slide against his as she found her footing. Morgan instinctively put his arms around her and felt a joy that he had never known. They stood there, two young people experiencing the ecstasy of first love, forgetting past lessons about proper behavior and the compassionless war that had brought them together. Without words being said, he kissed her warm and willing lips.

Some time later, with long shadows proclaiming the waning of day, Morgan broke the spell. "We'd better be getting back. There'll be concern about our being gone so long, and so late in the day."

"Yes, I know," Charity said. "But I wish we could be together like this forever. Darling, will we be together—forever someday?"

"Yes! Yes, my love, some way, God willing, we will be."

CHAPTER 9

As the days passed, the love between Morgan and Charity grew and intensified. They both knew that he would soon have to go back the war, and they made no plans, other than to try and enjoy each other's company as long and as often as possible. Several times the subject of his returning to the war came up, and each time one or the other would change the subject so as not to put a damper on their joy of just being together.

Morgan decided it would be proper for him to talk to her father about coming back after the war, but before he could do so, his world changed.

One morning after breakfast, Charity took one of her favorite books out to the big front veranda and made herself comfortable in one of the large, white wicker chairs that were always so inviting. Finding it difficult to read, she put the book aside and just sat there, relaxing and listening to the many pleasant sounds around the plantation. She soon observed two of the yard boys looking and pointing down the shady lane that lead directly away from the house to the main road. She looked in the same direction but at first could see nothing. Then she saw what had aroused their attention. She watched as a dozen horsemen rode up the lane toward the house. She dispatched one of the yard boys to get her father and continued to watch the approaching riders. She was soon relieved to see that they were dressed in gray. Although the lead rider's uniform lacked the fancy adornment that most Southern officers preferred, she instinctively sensed that he held a high rank. Riding straight and tall in the saddle, he rode a large bay stallion that displayed the gait of a Tennessee walking horse. To her, he was a striking example of what she thought a warrior should look like.

The riders stopped at the hitch rail, and all but the leader stayed in their saddles. He stepped down from the saddle and walked up the brick walkway, stopping near the steps leading up to the veranda. He removed his wide-brimmed hat and held it to his chest as he bowed to Charity. It was then that she recognized him as the general who had come to see Morgan several months earlier. She felt a sudden rush of anxiety as she realized this was the time she had been dreading.

"Good mornin', ma'am. Do you remember me, Bedford Forrest?"

"Good morning to you, sir. Yes, I do remember you. Welcome back to Honeywood."

At that time the door opened behind her, and her father walked across the porch and stood at her side. "Greetings, General. Let me join my daughter in welcoming you back to our home."

"Good morning, Thomas. I'm here to see Morgan Montgomery. Is he about?"

"I believe he's out walking with my son, but I'm sure they'll be back soon. If it's urgent, I'll send someone for them."

"That ain't necessary, sir. We don't mind waitin'. It'll do us good to stay out of the saddle for a short spell." He turned to his men and directed, "Dismount, men, and rest your tired bones a spell."

"Won't you and your men come in?" Thomas invited. "I'll have food prepared for you."

"That sounds mighty good," Forrest replied. "It's been a while since we've had a home-cooked meal."

"Well, you're about to have one now, and I'll have your horses fed and watered."

Two hours later, all the rebel horsemen had been well fed and were relaxing on the front veranda. Morgan and Charles had just returned, and Forrest was talking to Morgan. "Well, my boy, how you feeling now? You're looking fit."

"I'm feeling very good, sir," Morgan replied. "I've been doing a lot of walking to get my strength back. I've even been helping out with some of the work around here."

"Are you ready to get back to the fightin'?"

"Yes, I suppose I am, sir."

"I have good news for you. No more trumping through the mud to the battle. I've arranged for you to join my cavalry regiment. You're gonna be ridin' with me."

"That's great!" Morgan replied with much enthusiasm. "Thank you, sir. I'll try to serve you well."

At that time Thomas joined the general and the newly assigned cavalryman. "Morgan, we're all going to miss you around here. We consider you almost a part of the family. The general has told me that you're going with him, and that you must ride soon. In anticipation of your pending departure, I've had two new uniforms made for you. You'll find them in your room. You'll also find other necessary items you'll need, packed in saddle bags."

Morgan thanked Thomas, excused himself, and went up to his room to change into one of the new uniforms. In a few minutes he was back, looking like a true Confederate. "You look mighty spiffy. I'm afraid you're gonna make the rest of my men look like a motley crew," Forrest joked.

"I've picked out a good mount for you," Thomas said to the young man. "It's the gray tied at the end of the hitch rack. He's all saddled and ready to ride."

"There's no way I could ever thank you enough, or repay you and your family for your graciousness and hospitality."

"Just seeing you well and able again is ample payment. As far as the horse and saddle, consider that a small contribution to the cause. Now, my boy, Charity would like to see you. You'll find her at the rose gazebo."

"Thank you, sir," Morgan replied. Turning to Forrest, he said, "May I have a few more minutes, General? I won't be long." Forrest nodded his approval, and Morgan turned and ran down the brick walkway that led to the rose gazebo. A rush of memories came to him as he thought of all the happy hours he had spent there with Charity in the past few weeks. The profusion of red and yellow roses gave off a pleasing fragrance that enhanced the bitter sweetness of the moment.

Charity was waiting for him inside the gazebo. Morgan took her in his arms and then pushed back a little. "Charity, We've both known this time was coming, but I'm not at all ready for it. I don't suppose I would ever be ready to leave you. I love you so much, and God willing, I will come back to you and will ask you to marry me. Under these circumstances I can't ask for a commitment, and I can't give one, other than to promise that I will return if I'm able."

"Oh, Morgan, I love you with all my heart and I promise to be waiting for you, no matter how long it takes—and I will say yes."

Morgan saw that her lips were quivering and knew that she was fighting to hold back the tears. He tenderly embraced the most wonderful girl he had ever known, giving her a lingering good-bye kiss. His heart was breaking, and he could say no more. He simply turned and walked away.

With tears now streaming down her cheeks, Charity watched as he hurriedly walked back down the brick-covered walkway, and quickly disappeared around a clump of flowering shrubs at the corner of the house. Soon she heard the clip-clop sound of several horses being ridden down the lane. Morgan was gone.

In late afternoon of the same day, the little band joined the main body of Forrest's cavalry. The regiment then rode until almost nightfall, and when they came to the banks of the Big Black River, they made camp for the night. After the horses had been properly cared for and the men had eaten, Forrest sent for Morgan. "Young man, let me welcome you to this regiment. You're joinin' up with some of the best horsemen in the South. Guess I don't really know you very well, but I know the man who raised you, and that's enough for me. I believe you'll do honor to the name of John Newton and to this regiment."

At this point, Forrest stopped talking long enough to walk over to a makeshift desk and pick up a brown leather saddle bag. He opened one of the flaps and withdrew a handmade cigar, which he lit over the glass chimney of an oil-burning lamp. After a couple of puffs on the cigar he continued. "Morgan, I ask a lot of my men. You'll ride till you think you're growed to the saddle. You'll fight when you think you're too tired to stay in the saddle. You'll fight when you haven't had a bite to eat in two days. You'll fight when you're outnumbered two or three to one. You'll have more ridin' and fightin' ahead of you than you could've ever dreamed of, but you'll be doin' it all for a good cause. You'll be doin' it for the freedom of the South."

Forrest paused long enough to take a deep draw from the cigar. "I saw you ridin' beside Sergeant Dan Tucker this afternoon. You can't go wrong by sticking to him for a few days; he's one of my best men and he'll guide you straight. I'll ask him to help you learn our ways. Now, my boy, go back out there and get some rest. It'll be boots and saddle before first light."

Morgan was soon painfully aware of the accuracy in Forrest's description of what to expect. He had not ridden in months, except for the short rides around Honeywood. During his first full day in the saddle, they traveled more than forty miles. That night, when all the others were seated around one of several large campfires, he chose to stand until time to crawl into his bedroll, which didn't come any too soon for him.

"Get up! Get out of that bedroll! It's time to ride. You'd better grab some quick breakfast if you want any. We'll be ridin' in thirty minutes." Morgan rubbed his eyes and looked around to see that the voice was coming from Sergeant Dan Tucker. "I know you had a hard day yesterday, but everybody else is up and around."

Morgan got to the cook tent just as it was being disassembled, but he was in time to get a hot cup of coffee, a couple of thick slices of bacon, and a slice of sourdough bread. In twenty minutes he had his horse saddled and ready to ride.

"Ain't always fun, but it's better'n bein' a mud soldier." They had been riding for more than an hour, and that was the first thing Sergeant Tucker had said to him since rousting him out of a deep sleep. Tucker was a large man, standing over six feet tall and weighing two hundred pounds. Neither his reddish-brown hair—which Morgan thought was the color of the red hens in which Sissy, the Oakmont cook, had taken so much pride—nor his darker beard looked as if they had been trimmed in a year. His voice was very gruff, but there was an ever present smile on his face that made him look gentle. Morgan knew that he was going to like the man and that he would learn much from him.

For three days they moved around, never encountering the enemy and never spending more than one night in the same place. When Morgan asked Tucker why they seemed to be going around in circles, the sergeant explained, "It's just the general's way of keeping the enemy confused. We hit 'em where they don't expect us, and then we run, hide, and hit 'em again. Old Grant keeps a couple of regiments out looking for us all the time. Has had a whole brigade after us for a while, but he finally called half of them back to the fightin' at Vicksburg. Forrest don't know much about the book kind of fightin', but he always outsmarts the best the Yankees have to send after us. Just be patient. There'll be enough fightin' to go 'round, and then some."

That very day Morgan got his first taste of fighting as a cavalryman. Forrest ordered the enlisted men to dismount and rest the horses while he met with the officers and sergeants. In a short time Sergeant Tucker came from the meeting with word that they were about to go into action. He said that scouts had brought a report that a convoy of enemy supply wagons had been spotted leaving the railroad yards at Canton and heading in the general direction of Vicksburg. The little task for the day: capture the wagons and destroy everything that couldn't be carried away on horseback.

The job proved to be relatively easy. There were nineteen wagons escorted by a company of cavalry. Carbine and pistol fire was brisk at first, but the Yankees realized the futility of resisting when the screaming and yelling rebels rushed them with wild and reckless, devil-may-care abandon. The drivers jumped from the wagons and ran into some nearby woods. The mounted troops turned and headed for parts unknown. Five of the enemy were killed, and seven, including a colonel, were captured. It was all over as quickly as it had started. Forrest didn't like to be bothered with prisoners, and so the colonel and his six men were paroled, without horses or guns.

The food was much better than usual that night. After everyone had eaten his fill, Forrest personally knocked the bung from a cask of rum, saying, "Men, we have here a most generous gift, a cask of good Jamaican rum, handed over to us by the Yankees this very day. Anyone who's old enough can drink what you can handle. If you ain't old enough, or if you ain't so inclined, just help take care of the rest. Boots and saddle at first light."

Forrest did all of his fighting in Mississippi, Tennessee, Kentucky, and Alabama. His natural skill at raiding behind Union lines, destroying railroads and storage facilities, and taking all that was necessary to sustain his men and animals made him well-known to both friend and foe. Time and time again he had been given impossible tasks to perform, and he continually proved himself worthy of the highest praise from his superiors. He considered no mission too difficult for the hard-riding, hard-fighting men who rode with him.

Life in the Confederate cavalry was anything but boring. There were times when Forrest would give them a few days to rest and recuperate, but most of the time they were on the move. If they were not heading for a deliberate clash with the Yankees, they were moving to stay hidden from them.

Morgan sometimes thought the war was little more than a game to General Forrest. The general planned his every move like a well-played chess game, whether on the attack or in retreat. He always had scouts out roaming the countryside, looking for any and all signs of Yankee activity. He studied whatever local maps were available, and combined with the scouting reports, he often knew the local area about as well as the people who lived there. This, along with an abundance of common sense, usually gave him a distinct advantage over his Yankee adversaries.

One such case was the time Forrest played cat and mouse with a Yankee major who, two months earlier, had taken it upon himself to hang five of Forrest's scouts instead of holding them as prisoners. The men had not been in full uniform because they did not have full uniforms, and that had been used as an excuse to hang the men as spies.

Forrest picked out five wagons that had been captured the previous day, selected drivers for each one, and ordered twenty mounted men, including Morgan, to escort the wagons on the road toward Canton. They were given orders not to resist if they were discovered by a Yankee patrol. They started an hour before dark. Just as the sun was disappearing behind a bank of red clouds in the western sky, they were surrounded by about a hundred Union cavalry. A big, red-faced major yelled out in a gruff voice, "You drivers get down from them wagons. You riders dismount and stack arms, and you'd better make haste or you're dead men." As soon as Morgan and the others had obeyed orders, the major continued to berate them. "You stupid rebs really thought you were outsmartin' us, didn't you? Tryin' to move them wagons at night. Ain't no Reb alive that can outthink, outdrink, or outfight Major Booker T. Winston."

At that time a Union sergeant called the major's attention to the fact that the wagons had Union markings on them. "All right, you thieves, where'd you get them wagons? What unit are you with?" No one answered. "I'm gonna have every one of you mangy rebs shot if you don't answer. Now, who is your commanding officer?"

"I am!" boomed a voice from out of the shadows, "and if there's some shootin' to be done, it's gonna come from me and my men. You're surrounded by five hundred armed men. Now, throw all them guns on the ground and put your hands up, or there ain't gonna be a one of you standing when it's all over." Then out rode General

Nathan Bedford Forrest himself, and from the shadows in every direction came five hundred men.

"This is a dirty, low-down trick," the major grumbled.

"War's all dirty, Major," Forrest replied.

The major stared for a moment at the man who had just captured him and then blurted out, "You're Forrest, that Southern trash I been hearing about. I'll tell you one thing right now: you didn't outsmart me, you're just lucky."

"Ain't no luck to it," Forrest answered. "I've been lookin' for you for more'n two months, ever since you hung five of my men, the ones you captured in Jackson. No trial. Just hung 'em."

"I don't know what you're talking about. Ain't never hanged no rebels."

"You forgot that two of my men got away during the hangin'. They told me all about it. How two of the young ones begged for their lives while you laughed and personally ran the horses from under 'em. My scouts have covered a lot of turf lookin' for you. They rode in yesterday and reported seeing you camped near this road, and I knowed I had you."

"What you gonna do with us?"

"I'm aimin' to parole your men. As for you, you claim to be so smart; I'll let you figure that out." In quick reaction to those words the major turned, ran between some of his men, jumped on a nearby horse, and attempted to escape. He never reached the outer circle of men before being struck by more than a dozen rifle and pistol balls. The other Yankees were released unarmed, unharmed, and on foot.

Morgan felt a slight resentment toward Forrest for having used him and the others as bait for his trap, but he believed that Forrest would even use himself in the same manner to achieve his purpose. He often wondered what Forrest had really intended to do with that Yankee major, but he always assured himself that the man would have surely been turned over to military authorities for imprisonment. Morgan developed much admiration and respect for the diamond in the rough named Forrest, a man who became known to the armies of both sides as the Wizard of the Saddle.

Morgan spent much of his free time reminiscing about his relatively short stay at Honeywood Plantation—and Charity McLauren, the girl who had awakened emotions and feelings he had never experienced in his young life. During the last few weeks there, he had spent most of his waking hours in the company of the girl with whom he had fallen so deeply in love, and now he only had the memory of the sheer ecstasy he had so often experienced just being near her. His lips still tingled when he recalled that last lingering, blissful kiss in the rose-entwined gazebo. There were several letters from Charity over the first few months he had been back in the fighting. He sometimes received them weeks after they had been dated, but that was reasonable, considering the way he had been moving around. He wanted them, even if they were months old, as long as they kept coming. But they didn't.

He had been away from Charity about six months when the letters stopped. He grew quite concerned when several weeks passed, and then months, without a single letter. He was overjoyed when a carrier caught up to them with a large bag full of mail. There were three letters addressed to Morgan: one from the Newtons, written four months earlier, and two from Charity, written three days apart but more than two months before they arrived. He had bittersweet feelings while he read and then reread the letters. Each letter contained several dried rose petals. The fragrance reminded him of that last morning at Honeywood. As he read the letters over and over, looking again at the dates, he became increasingly concerned that something was wrong. He considered asking for permission to go to her, but having seen others denied requests of a much more urgent nature, he did not. He could only wait. He had a war to fight. Each night he prayed that Charity would be safe and that he would someday be with her again.

On July 4, 1853, Confederate Generals Pemberton and Bowen surrendered their forces at Vicksburg to Grant's Union army. This saved many a Southern boy from starvation, but it released more Yankee troops from their duties at Vicksburg, allowing them to establish other strongholds throughout the Deep South. However, General Forrest saw this as providing greater opportunities for him and the brave men who rode with him to engage and whip the enemy.

Music was a large part of every soldier's life during the Civil War. Many of the old songs were popular on both sides, and many songs were made up or added to as they were passed along from one unit to another. Morgan didn't know where one cavalry song came from, but he often thought of a single verse at the start on a mission:

> *Come tighten your girth and loosen your reins,*
> *Come buckle your blanket and holster again.*
> *Check the click of your trigger, and balance your blade,*
> *For he must ride sure that goes riding the raid.*

CHAPTER 10

From the beginning, Morgan demonstrated great leadership ability as Forrest handed the Yankees an almost daily dose of havoc and disorder. In less than three months from the time he joined Forrest's cavalry, he was assigned the rank of sergeant. By closely observing Forrest's every move, he quickly learned and adapted to the unconventional tactics and methods used by his commander. He was soon leading small units of cavalry on diversionary raids, actions to make the Yankees think Forrest was in one place while he was actually destroying a railroad or supply depot in a different location.

On one occasion, Morgan led a scouting party into a section of north central Mississippi, west of the little town of Holly Springs. A local citizen had told Forrest that the Yankees had established a supply distribution center in the area, and so Forrest sent Morgan and a dozen men to check it out. They were mounted and moving toward their objective an hour before daylight. By midmorning they saw numerous horse tracks, but they had not seen a single person all morning, not even an occasional local citizen. As they got nearer to their objective, Morgan and his men moved more slowly, observing the surrounding countryside for any sign of Union soldiers.

Morgan suddenly gave the hand signal to stop. "Listen," he whispered to the other riders. "What do you hear?"

"I think I hear cannon fire, way off over there," one of them replied as he pointed toward the east. Each man quietly listened. Sounds of cannonade could be faintly heard as the breeze shifted, like distant thunder on a summer night.

"Men, we're too few to help, but let's try to get close enough to see what's taking place. Then I'll determine a course of action."

They cautiously made their way down a small road toward the distant rumbling. They were close enough to hear the small arms fire when they spotted a large unit of Yankee cavalry, three or four hundred strong, approaching the road from the right but still several hundred yards away. The Yankees apparently saw the rebels at the same time and charged toward them at a full gallop. Morgan quickly observed a swamp with thick vegetation to their left, making it impossible to turn in that direction. He had only two choices: turn and run, or charge toward the sounds of heavy fighting. He chose not to run away. They charged toward the sound of battle. As they came closer to the fighting, Morgan could see men in trenches— men in gray.

The Yankee horsemen, who were now behind them, had apparently been sent to flank the several hundred well-entrenched rebels, but Morgan and his small band had spoiled their surprise. In a desperate effort to stop the fleeing rebels, the Yankees began shooting, but Morgan and his men were out of range of the Yankee carbines. Morgan's horse suddenly went down, sending the young sergeant sprawling through a patch of tall weeds and onto the hard, dry ground. One of his men came riding back, but Morgan waved him on. He got to his feet and ran for the cover of a nearby trench. Helping hands quickly pulled him into the relative safety of the freshly dug trench.

Several of the Yankee horsemen fell to the marksmanship of the fortified riflemen. With the help of some alert cannoneers on a nearby ridge, the rebels repelled the mounted assault.

Morgan was angry with himself for getting into his present situation. He had failed to complete his mission, he had been separated from his men, and he had lost his horse. He told himself that everything had happened so quickly that he really had no other course of action.

When the last Yankee was out of range, a tall, lanky major made his way through the trench to where Morgan had taken cover. "I'm Major John Stillwell of Reed's Louisiana Brigade. What's your unit?"

"I'm Sergeant Morgan Montgomery. I ride with General Forrest's cavalry—that is, I guess I did until I lost my horse."

The major gave a slight laugh at Morgan's subtle humor as he shook the sergeant's hand. "We're about ready to fall back to a better position. You might as well stay with us till it's over. We can use every man we can get."

One soldier crawled out of the trench and retrieved the carbine Morgan had lost when his horse fell. "This short gun ain't as accurate as the ones we shoot, but I guess you're use to it."

Morgan thought it best to remain with this unit until he had a chance to return to his own.

At the last minute, Major Stillwell decided not to move the unit because they had withstood the Yankees very well at their present location. One of the soldiers shared some of his hardtack with Morgan, which was only a little better than having nothing to eat. Morgan hunkered down against the side of the trench and tried to get ready for a long night. He was amazed at how quiet things became after dark. He could hear the sound of insects and an occasional bird call, but very little talk from the many men with whom he was sharing the trench. He supposed that they were too exhausted from the previous day's fighting to talk. He didn't think he could sleep under those conditions, but he was a little surprised when he awoke as the sun rose.

The next day was hot and dry. Early in the afternoon huge cumulus clouds towered on the horizon but dissipated without bringing rain. There were several small skirmishes throughout the day, with neither side showing signs of capitulating. The Yankees charged the rebel lines several times, and just as many times the rebels met them in the open field beyond the breastworks, often in hand-to-hand fighting. Hundreds of dead lay scattered across the large rolling meadow, like a dirty patchwork quilt with mixtures of green and blue and gray and red.

During lulls in fighting, Morgan tried to relax but with little success. He was concerned about his men after they were separated the previous day. He thought he had seen one of his men killed during one very brutal onslaught that morning, but he was sure that most of them had escaped the Yankee cavalry and had made their way back to Forrest.

There was little wind to ease the relentless heat. His eyes and lungs burned from the dense smoke that had been increasing all morning and persistently hung in thick layers like morning fog. At times it became almost impossible to breathe. Near nightfall the Union forces received reinforcements in the form of a full brigade of fresh troops. Word was quickly passed down the rebel line for everyone to fall back and make a stand in the woods behind them. They fell back, but no stand was made. The blue wall of humanity charged with such noise, and in such superior numbers, that the rebels never slowed down when they reached the woods. Morgan first attempted to stop some of the routed soldiers, but after realizing how futile his efforts were, he turned and ran with the others, away from certain death.

The wind came up, but instead of clearing away the smoke, it seemed to intensify it. The farther Morgan ran, the denser the smoke became. Then the thought came to him that he was no longer smelling the sulfuric odor of burned gunpowder, but smoke from burning wood. Several small grass and brush fires had erupted during the day, though most of them had burned themselves out.

With Yankee soldiers following close behind, Morgan began angling off to his right in the hope of getting around the source of the smoke, but it only got thicker. Large black particles of soot began to fall around him, some still glowing from the fire that had produced them. The air became uncomfortably hot, and he began to hear a loud roar ahead and to his left. He realized that he was caught between several thousand men who wanted to kill him and a raging forest fire. He could now see the flames as high as the treetops and hear the popping of small bushes exploding from the heat. He pondered whether he should keep running toward a fiery death, or give himself up to the enemy. He reasoned that he would probably be shot by the first Yankee who saw him coming back through the smoke and decided to keep running at right angles to the fire with the hope of outrunning it. It was no use. He could now see the inferno ahead as well as to his left. He told himself that his time had finely run out. Fleeting thoughts of Charity passed through his mind, and his greatest regret was that he would never see her again.

Suddenly he found himself with nothing under his feet. Then he hit face down in shallow water. He tried to get a breath of air but became strangled as he pulled water into his lungs. Coughing and struggling for life itself, he managed to get to his knees and get his head out of the water. For a short time he could not control the coughing, but his breath slowly as came back. Darkness had come from both the lateness of the day and the dense smoke, but the fire gave off enough light for him to see that he had fallen into a small stream. The water was only two feet deep, but the banks were at least six feet high. The heat was becoming unbearable. He was having great difficulty in breathing, and every muscle in his body ached from exhaustion. He made no attempt to climb out of the stream bed. Instead, he took his coat off and held it down in the water, making sure it was completely wet. He then placed it over his head and submerged the rest of his body in the water. Leaning back against the bank, with a small outcrop of rock over his head, he lost consciousness.

The next thing he remembered was someone pulling the coat from his head. It was morning, most of the smoke had cleared away, and the air was cool. "Stand up, Reb, and let's see if you're cooked about well-done." A man wearing a dirty blue coat, holding a big musket in one hand and Morgan's charred coat in the other, stood over him as he spoke. Morgan tried to stand but was unable to do so. The man threw the soot-covered coat on the sand at the edge of the water and stood his musket against the bank, well clear of the water. He took Morgan by the arm and helped him stand, giving him support for a few minutes. "Man, I don't see how you lived through that fire. We've found at least two dozen burned rebs scattered through the woods," the Union soldier said. He saw that Morgan's legs were about to give out and suggested, "Maybe you'd better sit down on that little sand bar for a few minutes. Aw, don't worry, I ain't gonna kill you. Anybody who could live through that hell last night sure don't deserve to be shot … and you sure ain't worth takin' prisoner."

After a few minutes, Morgan attempted to get up again, but he still had no strength. The man in blue laughed softly and said, "We'll be pullin' out of here soon, so you better stay here for a while. Some of my friends might want to use your worn-out carcass for target practice." He handed Morgan a canteen. "There's lots of dead men and horses upstream from here, some of them in the water, so you'd better keep this until you get out of here. I've got an extra canteen, so I'll leave this one with you. If I was you, I'd stay put for an hour or two before tryin' to get outta here."

"Thank you, and God bless you," was all that Morgan could think to say to the kind Yankee who had spared his life. He learned something when he first entered the war that had been reinforced many times since: both sides had many good, decent men who were fighting for what they believed to be the right cause. This was not the first time he had received compassionate treatment from an enemy soldier, and he hoped it wouldn't be the last.

The sun was now high enough for its warming rays to reach the bottom of the deep gulch. Chilled from being in the water all night, Morgan positioned himself against the bank, letting the sun warm his body. He soon fell asleep. He did not awaken until late in the afternoon.

Holding on to a root that was growing out of the bank, he pulled himself up to a standing position. Everything was quiet; he could not even hear a bird. He was pleasantly surprised that most of his strength had returned. He looked around for his musket or any other possession that he might have lost when he fell into the stream. He only saw the blackened coat that was no longer worth picking up. He slowly made his way down the streambed to a place where the bank was only about three feet high and climbed out.

He remembered that he had earlier lost his carbine and had thrown his pistol down during the heat of battle after an incoming minie ball had jammed the cylinder. He had fought the rest of the day with a dead soldier's musket, which he had now lost. As a cavalryman without a horse, and now without a weapon, he had no idea which direction to go. He started walking back in what he thought was the direction of the previous day's fighting. He soon came across a road that was deeply rutted by wheeled vehicles. There were hundreds of hoof marks and human tracks visible in the loose dirt, all going in one direction. He reasoned that the last ones over the road would have been the enemy, and he immediately turned around and started walking in the opposite direction. He soon came to a smaller road that intersected the road on which he was traveling. Actually, it was little more than a trail and appeared to be little used. His better judgment told him that it would be safer to get off the well-traveled road he was on. He turned south and continued walking.

It was nearing sundown when he came upon a clearing and saw a small farm house, weather-beaten and old. He opened the sagging gate and walked down the small path that led to the house. He stepped up on the creaking porch and knocked on the door. There was a slight rustling sound inside, but no one answered his knock. Knowing that most of the civilians in the area were frightened of anyone who approached their home, he turned, stepped off the porch, and walked down the path past the yard gate. The last thing he wanted to do was to further complicate the lives of the poor souls who lived there by insisting that he be let in. Looking back he saw a slight motion at one of the windows. Then the door opened a few inches and an almost childlike female voice called out, "Which side you on, mister?"

"The South," he yelled back, and watched as the front door opened a little wider.

"Come back a little closer, so's I can see for myself." He walked slowly back toward the front porch. When he got to within a few feet of the steps the person inside said, "That's close enough." A young woman, who appeared to Morgan to be seventeen or eighteen years old, stepped out of the doorway holding an antiquated shotgun. Her face was tan from days of working outdoors, and her long brown hair was sun-bleached at the ends. She was wearing a faded cotton dress and no shoes.

She raised the weapon until it was pointing directly at his chest and asked, "Why you out here by yourself? You a deserter?"

"I was in the battle that was fought east of here during the last two days. I'm sure you heard the guns."

"I been hearin' big guns all right, off over yonder," she said.

"I got separated from my men, and I'm trying to get back to them. I was hoping someone here could give me directions, or maybe tell me where the Confederates are bivouacked."

"I guess you're who you say you are. You look about like my husband did the last time he come home, with them dirty, ragged clothes and all. Ain't seen him in more'n six months." She stared at him for a short time, and he at her, neither knowing exactly what to say.

"Say, mister, you hungry?"

"Yes, I guess I am. I don't remember when I last ate. Must have been two or three days ago, except for some hardtack two nights ago. But I wouldn't want to put you to any trouble."

"Won't be no trouble. Ain't much, though. Got some cornbread, greens, and onions. Sit down on them steps, and I'll bring you a plate."

Morgan eased his weary body down on the porch steps and waited. It wasn't long before the young lady returned carrying a dented old tin plate on which there was a large portion of cooked greens, fried potatoes, and a hefty slab of cornbread. She also brought an oversized cup of water. Morgan thought of Sissy, the cook back home at Oakmont, whose favorite dish had been cooked greens.

As he ate, Morgan occasionally glanced up at the girl. She had at first appeared to be very plain and almost homely, but now he could see a strange kind of attractiveness about her, almost a hint of beauty, as she stood leaning against the doorway, watching him eat.

Morgan had consumed most of the food when she spoke. "My name's Georgiana Poke."

"Hello, Georgiana Polk. I'm Morgan Montgomery from Tennessee," he said in a lighthearted way.

"Well, Mister Morgan Montgomery from Tennessee, I reckon we've now been proper introduced. I wish I'd had better fixings to offer you. Wouldn't've had the cornbread if the wheel hadn't come off one of them army wagons over near the crossroads. They had to unload everything to fix it and left a barrel of cornmeal behind. The old man who lives across the woods a ways found it and brung me a portion of it."

"It's a wonderful supper, Georgiana. And thanks to the army, your neighbor, and especially to you for the good cornbread. I can't remember when I've had better."

"You sure say nice things. It does a woman real proud to have a man enjoy her cooking like that and tell her about it, even if it wasn't nothing but greens, taters, and cornbread. I sure miss having my man around to cook and fix for. I get powerful lonesome out here without nobody to talk to when day's done. And I'm always scared. I get so scared some nights I can't get to sleep at all. Don't guess there's much reason to be scared, seeing as how we ain't had any fightin' around here close until the last two or three days. Ain't no soldiers or nobody else ever comes around here, 'cept the old man what brung the cornmeal, bein' sorter out of the way like it is."

Morgan finished the food and placed the plate and cup on the edge of the porch near the steps. "I appreciate the hospitality, Georgiana. I've rested, and now I must be going."

Georgiana was quiet for a moment, and then with a little quiver in her voice she said, "Would you like to stay here tonight?"

In Morgan's mind there was no question as to her intent. The only question was of his resolve. He had lived among battle-hardened men, in the uncivil atmosphere of war for so long that he sometimes forgot his Christian upbringing. He had to always be alert against allowing his basic instincts to replace rational judgment. For a brief moment, he allowed raw nature to take over as tantalizing thoughts drove him dangerously close to giving in to the urges of his manhood. But before he passed that point of no return, better judgment did take control, and he heard himself say, "Georgiana, you'll never know how difficult it is to say no, but that's what I must say, and that's what I am saying. I'll leave now, because if I stay one minute longer, I'm apt to change my mind." He stood up and looked into her alluring eyes for a brief moment. "I hope things go well for you, and that your husband gets home real soon," he said. He turned and walked lively through the yard gate and onto the dusty little road that led away from her house, and he never allowed himself to look back.

CHAPTER 11

Morgan spent the night in a small thicket near the little-traveled road on which he had walked from Georgiana's cabin. The moon came out for almost an hour, and he was able to get three or four miles in before the sky became cloudy and near total darkness prevailed. He was having trouble even staying on the road, when a momentary break in the overcast allowed him enough moonlight to find the thicket in which to rest and hopefully sleep until morning.

Throughout most of the night, he struggled with his own personal demon. He could not put Georgiana out of his thoughts. It was not just the natural biological drive of young manhood; there was a genuine concern for her welfare. Would another soldier, placed in the same situation that had faced him only a few hours earlier, have had the common decency just to walk away from her? If the Yankees came to her house, would they show respect? Would her husband ever return to take care of her? He considered going back, but something in the back of his mind told him not to do so. Even though his love for Charity remained the essence of his endurance in the day-to-day rigors of war, he was afraid that he would not be able to resist the urges that were so new to him and so very strong. Slowly he began to draw strength from his faith from the religious teaching he had received during his adolescent years—lessons taught by his dear departed mother, his church, and in later years the

Newtons. He prayed that God would deliver him from further such enticements and would watch over Georgiana until her man returned to take care of her.

After finally falling asleep, he dreamed of a mighty battle where he was the only survivor. This was nothing new because he dreamed almost every night, and all of his dreams were about conflict and carnage.

He was awakened from a fitful sleep by distant voices. As he rubbed the sleep from his eyes, he saw pink-tinted clouds in the eastern sky. Somewhere nearby, a songbird exuberantly announced the arrival of a new dawn. He heard the voices again, fading away and then getting louder, and he could hear an occasional neighing of horses. He became quickly mindful that he was hearing the sounds of a military unit passing along the small road. He crawled to the edge of the brush, but there was not yet enough light to see anything but shadows. He grew concerned that he might be dangerously close to the enemy. Then someone with a genuine Southern drawl made a disparaging remark about a horse, and he knew he was safe.

"Hello on the road, I'm a friend," Morgan called out.

"Well, come on out, friend, and let's take a look at ye," said a flippant voice in reply.

Morgan could hear scuffing feet on the hard surface of the road as many men came to a halt. A horse snorted, and there was more scuffing of gravel as someone could be heard saying, "You no-good bag of worthless bones, quit a-jumping around 'fore I get off an shoot a hole in your worthless hide."

Morgan saw that only a dozen of the men were mounted as he stepped out onto the road directly in front of two men who were approaching him from among a shadowy column. Two long muskets with fixed bayonets were pointed directly at him. "Now, friend, tell us who you are and what you're doin' out here," one of the men demanded.

"I'm Sergeant Morgan Montgomery. I'm assigned to General Forrest's cavalry. I was on a scouting patrol when I lost my mount and got separated from my men a couple of days ago."

"What direction you headin'?" the man asked.

"Generally south. I don't know where Forrest will be now, but I stand a better chance of finding him if I move in that direction."

"We're what's left of Major Renfro's regiment. We're headin' south also, so you might as well move with us until you find your people. We can always use another man."

Morgan had heard that statement before—too many times. It seamed as though he could never stay with any one group of soldiers long enough to get to know any of them personally.

He agreed to travel with the regiment, happy to be in the presence of fellow Southerners. Someone handed him a long musket and the makings for twenty rounds, and orders were given to continue marching. As morning became light enough for him to observe all the men around him, he realized that he had joined the ragtag survivors of some hard-fought battles. Their uniforms were dirty and tattered, their shoes were in disrepair, and some were completely barefooted. Their tired, hollow-eyed faces suggested long periods without proper food and rest.

The man who had first questioned Morgan introduced himself as Captain Thomas Lewis, of Kentucky. "We're what's left of a regiment that had been reassigned to General Turner's brigade. While we were en route to join up with Turner, we got scattered all over the countryside. It was about a week ago when a Yankee division caught us by surprise as we bivouacked along the Tennessee River. They came at us before sunrise from all directions. They killed a lot of good men, including Major Renfro. We didn't have a chance to do anything but run for our lives. I managed to rally some of the stragglers together, and as we moved to the south, we picked up men from other outfits. We're short on everything but spunk and determination, but we'll soon join Turner, and things will be better, I hope."

Morgan was favorably impressed by the fact that most of the officers were walking; their horses were being used to carry some of the more seriously wounded. As he studied the poor souls around him, he thought of how fortunate he had been to this point. He had never been without proper clothing, and although he had known hunger pains, he had never gone more than a day or two without food. He was amazed at the good spirit and high morale of these destitute soldiers. One group would start singing, and soon the whole tattered regiment would join in. When they were not singing, he would often hear laughter break out as someone told a good joke.

Morgan was told that Captain Lewis had rationed their meager supply of food to only one meal a day, which was usually eaten after they had stopped for the night. That first night Morgan was glad to get a small portion of pan fried cornbread and a thin slice of salted beef (called salt horse by the troops), and hot brew that had a slight resemblance to the flavor of coffee. A tall boy who said he was from north Alabama told Morgan that the coffee, which he called stump water coffee, was made mostly from roasted acorns. He gave Morgan some molasses from a glass jar to help the flavor of the hot liquid. The small portion of food killed the hunger pains, but Morgan's stomach growled all night.

The next morning, there was plenty of stump water coffee but no food. They were on the road before daybreak. It was midmorning they were attacked by Yankee cavalry about two hundred strong. The riders came charging in from behind and from their right flank, shouting and yelling wildly as they fired their pistols and rifles and swung their short blades. The fray only lasted a few minutes, but when the riders retreated, seven rebels were on the ground, either dead or dying. Many of the standing survivors were bloodstained from injuries.

When they were on the march again, Morgan walked with Captain Lewis and asked, "What are they expecting to gain, attacking a unit this big with such a small troop?"

"I think it's just a way of harassing us and slowing our progress in joining up with Turner's brigade," the captain replied. "Several times during the last few days, small bands of Union cavalry have made short-lived attacks, forcing our men to take cover often killing or wounding a few of us. By the time we've taken care of the wounded and gotten reorganized, an hour or more has been lost."

The morning of Morgan's third day with the regiment, mounted scouts returned to camp with the news that General Turner's brigade had been located less than five miles away. They had made contact, and the general had sent word back that he would wait for them in camp.

To Morgan's delight, Turner's brigade was much better fed and equipped than the band of impoverished troops with which he had been traveling. That night he enjoyed a supper of fresh pork, cabbage, and baked cornbread. There had been a time when he would have considered that kind of nourishment to be no more than hog food, but now it was like manna from heaven.

Later that night, Morgan approached General Turner's aide-de-camp, Captain Abner McGee, and persuaded the captain to furnish him with a horse and supplies so that he could continue his search for Forrest's cavalry. The next morning, before most of the men had awakened, Morgan led his mount to the edge of camp and pulled himself into the saddle. He observed a few men standing around the smoldering camp fires but recognized none of them. He would liked to have said good-bye to a couple of the soldiers with whom he had traveled those last few days, but he knew it would be impossible to find them among so many men. There was enough light for him to see the dim outline of a road leading south out of camp as he urged his mount forward.

During the morning he saw a few people around some of the small farms he passed, but they all managed to disappear when they saw a stranger nearby. It was around noon when he came upon a farm that looked a little more prosperous than the others he had observed. In the front yard stood a farm wagon to which two horses were hitched.

As he rode up, a large man came out of the house and stood on the front porch. "Get down, young man, and rest a spell. You look a little saddle weary." The man extending the invitation was tall, although slightly bent and old, maybe seventy years of age or more. His white hair and beard were neatly trimmed and short.

"Thank you, sir," Morgan replied as he stepped from the saddle. "My feet haven't touched ground in more than six hours, and my horse is coming up a little gimpy in his right foreleg. I guess we both need a rest."

"I just came in from the field for dinner, and I think it's about ready. Will you join us?"

"Yes, sir. That is, if it won't be too much trouble."

"Shore won't be very fancy, but there'll be plenty, and it won't be any trouble at all." The man extended his hand as Morgan stepped up to the porch. "I'm Reverend Tucker."

Morgan introduced himself and followed his elderly host into the house. Although the reverend had said that the food wouldn't be fancy, Morgan considered it the best he had eaten since he left Honeywood. There was fried smoked ham, turnip greens, baked sweet potatoes, and oven-baked cornbread, all served with real coffee. When Morgan thought he could eat no more, Mrs. Tucker brought out a steaming peach cobbler. After dinner, Mrs. Tucker asked the two men to move out to the front porch while she cleared the table and washed the dishes.

The old man stopped and took a pipe and tobacco pouch from the fireplace mantel as they passed through the small, neat living room. After the two were seated in the two large rocking chairs on the front porch, Reverend Tucker packed tobacco into the bowl of the old pipe and lit it as he asked, "What brings you this way, Sergeant?"

I'm looking for my unit. I've been separated from it for several days. Have you heard of a large cavalry unit around this area recently? My commander is General Bedford Forrest."

"Well, glory be! My son rides with Forrest. You might know him—Sergeant Daniel Tucker."

"Sir, I'm privileged to know the father of Dan Tucker. Yes, I know him well. He's the one who took me under his wing and taught me most of what I know about surviving a war."

"How is he?" the old man asked. "When did you see him last?"

"I saw him the night before I rode out with a scouting party; let's see, that was several days ago. I've lost track of time. He was in good health then."

The old man called his wife out to tell her what Morgan had just related to him. The two were elated over word about their son and insisted that Morgan stay longer, but he told them that he must continue his search for his unit. Reverend Tucker then persuaded Morgan to take one of his saddle horses to replace his gimpy one.

With a full stomach, a good mount under him, and the warm autumn sun on his face, Morgan continued his search. Two days later he came across a regiment of Forrest's cavalry, commanded by Colonel Bell. He joined with Bell's regiment, and the next day they made contact with the main body of the brigade. Morgan learned that only three of the men from his scouting expedition had returned; the others were believed to have been killed or captured.

That night Morgan found Sergeant Dan Tucker and told him of the visit with Dan's mother and father. Dan was overjoyed to learn that they were well. Morgan showed Dan the horse Reverend Tucker had traded to him, and Dan said it was his father's most prized stallion. Morgan insisted that Dan take the horse for himself, which after much discourse, Dan agreed to do. Dan then became nostalgic and talked for hours about his family and growing up on a farm under the supervision of his preacher father. Morgan listened but said little. While Dan talked, Morgan's mind drifted back to his growing up years in Lewis County and at Oakmont. He wondered if someday he would be able to take up where he had left off.

CHAPTER 12

Nathan Bedford Forrest was born to a poor family in Chapel Hill, Tennessee. With a little luck, a lot of hard work, and several smart speculations, he had become a millionaire, one of the richest men in the South when the Civil War started. He returned to Tennessee after the war broke out, enlisted as a private in the Confederate Army, and trained at Fort Right in Randolph, Tennessee. In a short time he was promoted to the rank of lieutenant colonel and was authorized to recruit and train a battalion of confederate mounted rangers. To make sure the new men under his command were properly equipped, he purchased horses and necessary supplies with his own money.

Not long after his promotion, Forrest was assigned to the command of General Braxton Bragg. From the beginning there were many heated arguments between the two officers. Forrest made no attempt to hide the fact that he had little respect for his superior. Forrest considered Bragg to be arrogant, bull-headed, and totally incompetent He told some of his closest associates that Bragg knew the book but had little common sense for using what he knew.

Forrest, on the other hand, had little knowledge of formal military tactics but possessed a natural aptitude for out maneuvering the enemy. He once made a statement, "Show me a man who fights by rote, and I'll have him whipped before he pitches his tune."

Bragg often made public references to the fact that Forrest had no formal education and had not gone to West Point. Bragg, refusing to recognize the fact that Forrest had become one of the most successful officers in the Confederate army, let it be known that he considered Forrest unskilled and insufficiently trained to command in battle.

In October of 1863, Jefferson Davis decided that it was necessary to leave Richmond and go into the field to investigate the many complaints coming from Bragg's disgruntled subordinates. Among the things agreed upon during Davis's meetings with Bragg was that several of the officers would be reassigned to other units. As for Forrest, Bragg agreed that it was time to let the "hot-tempered" cavalryman go.

Forrest then arranged a meeting with Davis and obtained his consent to operate as an independent unit. He would concentrate his campaign, for the time being, in what was then referred to as the west, where he would be free to operate in and around the Union lines in northern Mississippi and western Tennessee. At that time Forrest had over four thousand men under his command, many of whom he had personally recruited, and many of whom were using mounts and equipment that had been purchased by Forrest's personal funds. Before Bragg released Forrest from his command, he managed to reassign most of the men in Forrest's brigade to other units, leaving Forrest with fewer than a thousand ill-equipped men.

It seemed that everyone wanted to ride with General Forrest, and two months later, Forrest's cavalry was back to near brigade strength with over three thousand men. Conscription officers from other units complained that Forrest's recruiters were always a day ahead of them in every town. The truth of the matter was that nearly every farm boy old enough to go to war had heard of Forrest's gallant leadership and audacious deeds, and the impressionable lads wanted to become a member of his cavalry.

After being freed from Bragg's command, Forrest had captured enough horses, food, warm clothing, and bedding, as well as arms and other equipment, to provide for the entire unit. He had even distributed extra animals and supplies to other Confederate units in the area.

On December 2, Morgan was summoned to General Forrest's command tent. When he arrived, there were several officers already present. "Morgan," Forrest said, "I ain't had much time to personally watch you in battle, but my officers tell me that on several occasions you've performed above and beyond what I expect of a sergeant. We need more men like you in our officer ranks. So I've decided, and everybody agrees with me, that you are now, at this time, promoted to the rank of lieutenant."

Forrest then instructed his acting aide-de-camp, Colonel Tyree Bell, to administer the oath of office without hesitation. After congratulations from all present, Forrest placed an arm around Morgan's shoulder and said, "Young man, I know John Newton would be proud to know how well you're doin'. I intend to dispatch a letter to him telling him all about you. And I'm also plannin' to give you leave to visit with John and Martha the next time we're near Columbia."

Christmas Day of 1863 was not a good day for Morgan. He had been given fifty men and assigned the job of guarding a long wooden bridge that crossed a rain-swollen creek a few miles east of Jackson, Tennessee. It was cold, and rain mixed with sleet fell throughout the day. It was almost impossible to have cook fires, and so food had to be eaten cold. As he ate beef jerky and hardtack and washed it down with water, Morgan's thoughts went back to the happy and festive Christmas days at Oakmont. He could almost smell the aroma coming from Sissy's kitchen as she and her helpers prepared Christmas dinner. The large dining table would be laden with the best that Oakmont had to offer. There would always be baked ham with applesauce, fried chicken, beef roast with brown gravy, and usually two or three other kinds of meat, plus a variety of vegetable dishes. The sideboard would be covered with at least a half dozen kinds of dessert. For some reason Morgan lost his appetite for the jerky and hardtack.

He thought of Charity and wondered what kind of Christmas they were having at Honeywood. He was not many miles from her, yet it might as well have been a thousand. In his mind he rode up to the magnificent home and found Charity standing by the hitch rail, waiting for him. He imagined the pure joy of taking her in his arms and kissing her long and tenderly. Then a strong gust of cold wind brought him back to reality, back to the war.

As night approached, he began to feel secure in the fact that a day had passed without the conflict of battle, a day without losing a single man to death or mutilation by an always persistent enemy. He sent for his two sergeants. Just as they arrived, large flakes of snow began to fall, replacing the rain and sleet. Visibility was quickly reduced to less than a hundred yards.

When the sergeants reported to him, Morgan said, "Boys, I've been told that it's urgent to hold this bridge. I was told that it will be needed tomorrow, and I was ordered to hold it at any cost. I want to have two shifts awake and alert at all times. Sergeant Johns, you and twenty-five men will have the first watch. You don't have to stand picket, but make sure every one of your men stays awake. Sergeant Hartsfield, you take the second watch. Just be sure to relieve Johns and his men at midnight, and make sure your men stay alert till morning."

He dismissed the sergeants and was looking in his haversack to determine how much food he had remaining when the startling sound of musket fire erupted from all directions. Both sergeants, who were not yet out of his sight, fell with the first volley. As Morgan made a dash toward the bridge and could see gray-clad soldiers falling all around him. Twice he felt minie balls tug at his clothing, but his body was not hit. He called for his men to fall back and take cover, but he could not hear his own voice over the intermingled sounds of screaming horses, dying men, and gunfire. As he attempted to take cover in a small ditch, he saw a Union cavalryman coming straight at him at full gallop, saber at the ready. The saber missed but the horse did not. Knocked several feet by the charging horse, Morgan lost consciousness before he hit the ground.

Some time during the night he became aware that he was cold and in pain. Slowly, memory of the union attack came to him, and he thought of his men. He remembered seeing many of them fall, but knowing there was nothing he could do in the total darkness, he pulled his coat tighter around him, drew himself into a fetal position, and hoped to survive the frigid winter night.

Morning finely came, and the dreadful battle arena had been transformed into a peaceful scene, draped in the gentleness of a fresh snowfall. With much difficulty, Morgan stood up, brushed the snow from his clothes, and surveyed the surroundings. He located the bodies of some thirty of his men but was unable to find a single living person. He knew the others had either been captured or driven away by the Yankees. And all the horses were gone. Upon inspection of the bridge, he determined it to still be useable, although an attempt had been made to burn it during the night.

Expecting a relief column at any time, he decided to wait near the bridge but out of sight. Light snow, which had continued to fall throughout the night, gradually changed back to sleet mixed with rain. On one of the dead horses he was delighted to find a bedroll containing a blanket and oilcloth outer cover. He promptly wrapped himself in first the blanket and then the oilcloth. In an attempt to get his mind off his present circumstances, he directed his thoughts to Charity and the happy times they had enjoyed together. He knew he would never experience another love like that which was now in his heart for Charity. He assured himself that she would be waiting for him when this crazy war came to some kind of conclusion. As he had so often done, he remembered every detail of his stay at Honeywood. He tried to reclaim every moment he spent there, beginning with when he first regained consciousness after being brought there. His first memories of the McLauren home were of the nice aroma and pleasant sounds coming from Sudie's kitchen.

His thoughts were interrupted by the sound of many horses breaking through the thick crust of ice that had formed on top of the snow. His stomach muscles tightened, and his heart began to beat wildly. Were the approaching sounds made by friend or foe? Ice had formed on the oilcloth and the grass and other vegetation around him. As he moved to take cover in a nearby thicket, small pieces shattered and fell to the frozen surface with the sound of breaking glass. The approaching riders soon came into view from around a grove of small pine trees. To Morgan's great relief, they wore the many shades of Confederate gray.

The detail of some sixty riders—under the command of a Captain Morrison, with whom Morgan had ridden on several raids—were ordered to dismount and take up picket positions on either side of the road. Morgan made his presence known to Captain Morrison, who soon set about checking the bridge while Morgan accompanied him. Both men agreed that the blackened timbers appeared to be strong enough to hold the heavily-loaded wagons that would cross when Forrest's brigade came that way.

While the two officers were discussing the condition of the bridge, a rider approached carrying orders to abandon the bridge and rush back to the main column. It had been decided that the bridge, defended at the expense of so many lives, was no longer needed. Despondent over the loss of so many comrades, and a little resentful that it now appeared to have all been in vain, Morgan had to fight back a flood of emotions. Without a mount of his own, he climbed up behind one of the cavalrymen to ride double. Like a good soldier, he was putting his feelings aside and returning to some yet-to-be-decided battle. They left behind the bodies of the dead, covered with a shroud of snow and ice. If possible, a burial detail would be sent back later.

By midmorning the temperature moderated to above freezing, and the sleet and freezing rain turned into a cold downpour of rain. The road became a loblolly of snow, broken ice, and mud, making it so slippery that the riders had to dismount and lead their horses, making progress extremely slow.

Near midday the road merged onto a wider road that had recently been traveled by a large mass of horses and many wagons. Captain Morrison decided to follow the direction of the large force. He dispatched a dozen riders to make sure they were not following the wrong column.

The ice and snow had been pulverized by the preceding unit, making the surface much rougher but travel much faster. After an hour on the larger road, one of the point riders returned at a gallop. He reported that they had found a couple of dozen dead Yankees along the roadside, where there appeared to have been a small skirmish. The rider also reported that they had caught a loose horse for Lieutenant Montgomery, if he didn't mind riding in a Union saddle. The main column was overtaken by late afternoon, and Morgan had his first hot meal in two days.

For several days that followed, cold rain and sleet continued to fall, and there was little activity from either of the armies. Forrest's men built large fires around the camp in an attempt to dry clothing and to and stay warm. Many had their blankets and oilcloths wrapped around their shoulders as they stood around the fires, warding off the bone-chilling cold. Sleeping tents had been set up, but they were cold and wet, as were the clothes and boots of all the men.

The free time, however, was a kind of blessing for General Forrest because it allowed him the opportunity to thoroughly inspect his brigade and evaluate its strengths and weaknesses. He required his officers to give a full accounting of all able-bodied men, animals, equipment, and supplies. He also had time to plan for new expeditions against the enemy.

He came to the conclusion that, for the next month or so, he needed to concentrate his efforts in the western sections of Tennessee and Kentucky. But first, he would make sure that his men were well prepared for some hard riding and hard fighting.

A few days into January, General Forrest sent for Morgan. Morgan entered the tent to find Captain Tom Rice, from Morton's artillery battery, and three artillery sergeants already present. Forrest was standing over a small portable table, writing something on a sheet of paper. "Gentlemen, find yourselves a seat," he said. "I'll be with you in a minute."

After a short time he turned, looked for a moment at the paper on which he had been working, and addressed the small group. "Men, I'm sending you five, along with sixty enlisted men, on a special mission. Tom, you'll be in charge of the mission, and Morgan, you'll act as his adjutant. I've lost a dozen pieces of artillery in the last few weeks: five captured by the Yankees, two when a bridge we was crossing washed out, and the others were abandoned someplace. I'm in bad need of replacements. Last spring we captured ten pieces near Edwards Station—five twelve-pounder howitzers, three ten-pounder Parrott rifles, and two twelve-pounder Napoleons. We didn't need 'em at the time, and so we hid 'em in an old, run-down barn and covered 'em with loose hay."

The general handed the paper to Captain Rice, waiting a moment for him to look it over. "I sure hope they're still there. That's what I'm sending you to find out. I've made a rough map of the area down there, and I hope my memory serves me well. You'll most likely have to scout around a little to find the barn, but this map will get you close. Men, I don't have to tell you it'll be a dangerous trip, because from what I hear, the Yankees are crawling all over that area. Reports say most of them are deployed in small scattered units, which will be to your advantage. You'll be takin' a six-horse team for each gun, so you'll be able to move fast, if need be. Bring 'em all back if you can, boys. If you can't bring 'em all, I'm countin' on you to at least bring the Parrott rifles and the howitzers. Now, better get yourselves a little rest, because I want y'all on the move well before first light."

There was little sleep for Morgan that night. Forrest had mentioned that the guns were hidden near Edwards Station, and Edwards Station was only a few miles from Honeywood Plantation, and Charity. But he knew he would not be able to leave the mission long enough to go there. It would be nothing less than desertion to ride away from such an important mission for personal reasons.

The rain had stopped during the night, and stars shone brightly in the night sky when the column of 65 men and 125 horses moved away from camp. But the clear sky was too good to last. By early afternoon the rain returned, bringing with it a strong south wind that drove cold rain directly into the faces of man and animal. Both the wind and the rain lasted for three days. The only redeeming aspect of this adverse situation was that they were able to travel all the way to Edwards Station without seeing a single Yankee.

By the end of the third day, the rain had stopped, the wind had subsided, and the only clouds in the sky were a few small, puffy ones. They made camp near the Canton Road, only a few miles north of Edwards Station. As they had done each night, they ate cold rations and bedded down for some much-needed rest.

Everyone was up and ready to ride by four o'clock the next morning. There was, however, one big problem. Forrest's map depicting the location of the old barn had gotten wet. The ink had run so badly that the map would be of no use at all. In order to expedite the search for the barn, they split into two groups that would rendezvous back at the campsite at nightfall. Morgan took one group consisting of himself, one of the artillery sergeants, and ten enlisted men. Captain Rice took the same number of men with him, leaving the rest to guard the extra horses.

Morgan and his men were to search the area east of an imaginary north–south line running through Edwards Station. They rode south until they came to a tall stand of pines. They stopped in the trees, and Morgan further divided his men into two details. He and the sergeant would each take five men. The sergeant and his men would search north of the Vicksburg-to-Jackson railroad, and he and his men would look south of the railroad. They would meet in the same pines in late afternoon.

After riding a half hour, Morgan's group came within sight of the railroad. Morgan sent one man to check the area for any sign of Yankees. The rider soon returned to report that the line was clear. They crossed the rails only a short distance from the place where Morgan had experienced his first taste of combat, and it brought back a flood of memories. A strange feeling came over him—not fright, but a kind of apprehension—as he remembered details of that morning when a full regiment of Grierson's Yankee cavalry ripped through camp and killed so many men, including Captain Gentry, as fine a man as Morgan had ever known. He soon regained his composure and continued with the job at hand.

The little band of rebels knew the enemy could be anywhere and were careful not to cross roads and open fields without thoroughly checking for danger. Once they spotted a mounted patrol moving down a narrow road, but they were able to stay hidden until the bluecoats had disappeared across a small ridge. During the course of the day, they checked several old barns, and some that were not so old, but without a hint of success. By late afternoon Morgan decided it was time to head back for the meeting with his other men. It had been a most trying day for him because throughout the day he had been intensely aware that he was only a few miles from Charity, and his heart ached because he could not go to her.

They arrived at the pine grove in late afternoon and found the artillery sergeant and his five men waiting. The sergeant reported that they had found nothing, and so they proceeded northward toward the campsite. The sergeant told Morgan that he and his men had not seen any sign of the enemy, but they had heard a short period of distant musket fire during the afternoon, and he believed it had come from a few miles southwest of where they were searching. The news made Morgan a little anxious, but he knew there were sure to be small bands of both Yankee and rebel units around the area, and it was inevitable that they would skirmish from time to time.

The little band arrived at camp a little before dark. The men who had been left to guard the extra horses appeared to be delighted to see them coming. Captain Rice and his men had not yet returned. After their horses had been cared for, Morgan advised the men to eat whatever cold food they had, because they would still not risk a cooking fire. The evening air was turning very cold. Morgan took the blanket from his bedroll and draped it around his shoulders while he waited in the darkness for the arrival of the captain and his men.

An hour passed, and then two. Then it was ten o'clock, and still no sign of his fellow soldiers. It was nearing midnight when the duty pickets came to Morgan and reported that a lone horse was coming toward camp from the south. Morgan could hear the other men moving around and knew that they were all awake. He whispered an order for everyone to stay low and remain quiet until the rider could be identified. There was enough light in the clear night sky to see the profile of the approaching horse and rider. "Halt! Identify yourself," Morgan called out. The horse stopped just as the rider fell from the saddle. Morgan rushed to the fallen man, struck a match, and saw that it was the sergeant who had ridden out with Captain Rice.

The sergeant was unconscious. One of the men stepped forward and said, "He's my brother; I'll tend to him." After a quick examination, the man stated, "He's been in a bad scrap. Been stuck two, no, three times with a saber. Lost a lot of blood."

The brother, with the help of two other men, wrapped the sergeant in a blanket and placed him on a bed of pine boughs in an attempt to make him comfortable. Knowing he could do nothing for the wounded man, Morgan decided that he should get some rest. He had not been in his bedroll long enough to get warm when a soldier brought word that the sergeant was talking. Morgan hurried to the man's resting place, and knelt at his side. "This is Lieutenant Montgomery, can you hear me?"

"Yes, Lieutenant, I can hear you," came an almost inaudible reply. "Message ... for you."

Morgan bent a little lower, putting his ear closer to the sergeant's face. "Go ahead, I can hear you, Sergeant. What's the message?"

"We found the guns, but it was a trap." The wounded man took several labored breaths before continuing. "Yanks must've been watching the barn, 'cause we were just startin' to look the pieces over, when ..." He stopped again to get his breath and did not continue for a full minute. "Came charging in from all directions. We all got killed, 'ceptin' me, and I'ma dyin'."

"You're going to be all right, Sergeant," Morgan assured him. "Can you tell me where you found the guns?"

"Yes, sir, I'll try. Follow the railroad two miles west of Edwards Station and then go south one mile. When you come to a deep gully, follow it to the right, and you'll come to the barn. It'll be a hundred feet to the right of the gully."

"That's enough talking for now," Morgan said. "Get some rest, and you'll be all right,"

"No, you ain't bein' exactly straight with me, and I know it. But listen to me, there's more. The cap'n said if any of us reached you, to tell you to get back to the brigade, quick time. Ain't no way you can take them guns. Yankees were …"

As the moon peeked through a hole in the clouds, lighting a small area around them, the sergeant died. The brother kneeled beside him and wept openly. "What will I tell Mama?"

CHAPTER 13

It was near midnight when a lone horseman rode away from camp. Only a few thin clouds remained in the sky, and a hunter's moon made it possible for man and horse to make good time down country lanes and through open fields, heading south toward the railroad and Edwards Station.

Before leaving camp, Morgan gave the remaining sergeant orders to take what was left of the unit back to rejoin the brigade. He also handed the sergeant a letter for General Forrest, a letter explaining the failed attempt to retrieve the much needed artillery pieces. It also stated that Morgan believed the enemy would now remove the guns and place them into service against the Confederates, as they were no longer of value as bait for a trap. He ended the letter by saying that he would try to find a way to keep the enemy from putting the guns into use.

Morgan had chosen not to bring anyone else with him. He was sure that a careful man, traveling alone, had a good chance of slipping around any patrols or pickets that might otherwise prevent him from carrying out his mission. Actually, he had no definite plan, other than attempting to find the barn and evaluating whatever situation he might find there.

He estimated the time to be around four o'clock when he came to the railroad just west of Edwards Station. Following the dead sergeant's directions, he turned right and rode west. When he believed he had traveled about two miles, he left the railroad bed and proceeded southward. He had traveled no more than a few hundred yards when he came to a well-traveled road that the sergeant had not mentioned. His memory of the area told him that it was the Jackson–Vicksburg road, and so he quickly crossed over and continued southward. New clouds had partially hidden the moon, and dawn had not arrived; the going was much slower now. At one point the horse came to an abrupt stop. Morgan tried to quietly urge him on, but the animal would not move. Morgan dismounted to investigate the horse's strange behavior. As he walked in front of the horse, he could see well enough to make out a four-foot-high rail fence across his intended path. He removed several of the rails and led the horse through the gap before remounting.

As he searched the area ahead for watch fires which might mark the location of enemy pickets, he kept the horse headed in a generally southern direction but allowed enough free rein for the animal to make its way in the darkness. Suddenly the horse stumbled, lost its footing, and slid down a steep grade. Morgan's reaction was to leap from the saddle to avoid being injured by the horse landing on him, but he was too slow to act. Both horse and man rolled and slid several feet, coming to a stop in a bed of gravel.

He had located the gully, but at what cost? The horse was noisily thrashing around on the ground, and Morgan's right outer thigh burned like someone had stuck him with a hot poker. He felt of his leg and found that his trousers were torn down the side. He also felt warm moisture and knew that he was injured enough to bring a flow of blood. Although hurting in several places, he stood up and found that everything worked. The horse stopped moving, and everything became very quiet. Morgan crawled to the horse and, finding its head, pulled on the bridle. In response, the head turned at a strange angle, and Morgan knew the animal was dead from a broken neck. There was nothing to do but make his way on foot down the gully, as the sergeant had directed. After several minutes of walking, the approaching dawn gave enough light for him to see the large barn, standing almost forebodingly on the little ridge above him. He observed the surrounding area for a few minutes but saw nothing to concern him. He found a small ditch that branched off the gully leading up the ridge toward the barn. Keeping low, he followed the ditch as far as possible before climbing out and proceeding across an open area. He was almost to the barn when a gust of wind rustled some dead leaves on an oak tree that stood near the barn. It was like some ominous warning because there had not even been a breeze before, and for a moment Morgan was unnerved. He then cautiously made his way to the oak and stood against its trunk for several minutes, evaluating the surroundings. Then, some thirty feet away, a dim glow caught his eye. From the experience of hundreds of nights of camping out, he recognized the glow as the remains of a fire from the night before. The sudden gust had caused a revival of the embers.

The dawn was now providing enough light for Morgan to see that there was no one near the fire. Only a few feet away he could make out an open side door to the barn. Remembering General Forrest saying that the guns had been covered with hay, he decided to make his way into the barn to investigate further. Inside, he moved away from the doorway and stood in the darkness to allow his eyes to adjust. The surface was soft and spongy, and he was sure that he was standing on a carpet of loose hay. After a few minutes of silent observation, he could make out several objects around the inside of the barn that appeared to be mounds. After further study, he decided that he was surely looking at the artillery pieces.

He was startled when a voice nearby whispered, "Andy, are you awake?"

Another sleepy voice answered, "Be quiet, Ralph, and let a fellow get some sleep. It's not even daylight yet."

Morgan froze in place. How many were there? It would be full light in another half hour. He couldn't stand there and let them find him—he had to do something soon, or it would be too late. In a low crouch, he slowly made his way back out the side door and to the leftover remains of last night's fire. He took a short stick from the edge of the ashes and smoldering coals. He blew hard on the glowing end of the dry wood, and it began to blaze. Holding the stick behind him to help hide the small blaze from anyone who might be looking around, he reentered the barn. But just as he passed through the doorway, there was another strong gust of wind, and the flame went out. He slowly crawled toward the center of the barn. A strong, cold wind began to rush through the barn. The old timbers cracked and groaned, and Morgan could hear people coming awake all around him. A dozen or more people must have been sleeping in the barn, each one a potential hazard to his health.

He crawled to one of the mounds of hay, and while remaining in a prone position and as close as he could get to the mound, he started blowing on the ember end of the stick. It glowed red and smoked, but there was no flame. He continued to blow until he became light-headed, but still no flame. He then held a handful of the loose hay to the end of the stick and continued blowing. That worked; a small flame appeared in the hay. He gave it a couple of seconds to catch the hay in the mound ablaze, and then he started making his way back toward the exit. The interior of the barn quickly became illuminated by the fire as it rapidly spread through the dry hay. Whipped by the increasingly strong wind that was finding its way through the old structure, the flames soon jumped ten feet high.

Morgan realized that it was no time to crawl on the floor. He had to get out of there, and fast. He jumped up and bolted toward the open door. As he started through, a large blue form stepped in front of him. It was the biggest Yankee Morgan had ever come face-to-face with. He hit the man in the midsection with all of his might, followed by an uppercut to the man's jaw as he bent over from the first blow. He felt something give and didn't know if he had broken his hand or the soldier's jaw. White-hot pain went through his fist and up his right arm, but the man went down with a thud. Morgan ran as fast as he could down the ridge toward the gully. As he ran, his right leg began to hurt, causing him to stumble and fall. He got to his feet and ran again. A dozen shots were fired from near the barn. Musket balls kicked up dirt around him, but he was not hit.

As he slid feet first into the gully, he heard someone back near the barn barking out orders. "Where you think you're goin'? Get back here and put this fire out. We'll catch that reb later."

Morgan moved as fast as possible down the gully until he came to a thick stand of small pine trees. As he climbed out of the gully, he looked back and saw a huge column of smoke rising from the direction of the barn. The sun was now rising, giving the smoke a curious orange hue. He entered the pines and decided he had to rest for a few minutes. His leg had bled a lot while he was running, but while he was resting it stopped. When he stood up he found that the leg was becoming stiff. He tried to walk, but the leg would no longer support him. He found a broken pine limb about two inches thick and six feet long, with a fork at one end. With his knife he notched the limb at the big end about four feet from the fork and managed to break it at the notch. He then cut the forked end to where he had about five inches on each fork. With his makeshift crutch, he headed southeast.

He had left his short carbine with the dead horse, but he only had a six-inch belt knife and his .44 caliber revolver, and he sure hoped that he didn't encounter the enemy. He was hurting, he was tired, and he was hungry. At that time he felt as though he never wanted to fight again.

Moving at a slow pace, he continued making his way toward the southeast, although he wondered if maybe he should be working his way back toward the north. Then it dawned on him that he was only a few miles from Honeywood. His subconscious must have been directing him, he thought to himself, and why not? He was not fit for combat, and he might not get another chance to see Charity before the war ended. He would go to Honeywood. The very thought of being near Charity made him feel better, and he ambled along a little faster.

He chose to make his way around the many large, open fields that lay between him and his destination. This made the journey much harder and more painful to his bad leg, but it helped cut down on the chance of being seen by some roving Yankee patrol. At noon he stopped to rest near a small stream. The temperature had dropped several degrees, and the strong wind made him shiver. He looked around for a safe place to rest and decided on a nearby patch of small oaks with thick underbrush. He raked together a large pile of oak leaves, and when his body sunk into the bed, the leaves almost covered him. Warmed by the dry leaves under and around him, he fell asleep within a few minutes.

When he awoke it was dark, and he was in trouble. Not a hundred yards away he could see the flames of a fire and hear the voices of several men. He watched and listened. The wind was still blowing through the surrounding trees, muffling the voices, and he could not make out what they were saying. The fire did not give off enough light to determine the color of their uniforms. Rather than take a chance on it being a Yankee camp, he decided to stay in his warm bed until the camp settled down to sleep, but he fell asleep first and did not awaken until well after daybreak the next morning. His attention was immediately drawn toward the camp, but he neither saw nor heard anything to indicate the presence of the previous night's neighbors.

He wearily got to his feet to get a better look. There was no one there; all he saw was smoke from a smoldering fire. Rebels or

Yankees, whoever had camped there, had obviously never known of his presence. His right leg was sore and stiff, but he was no longer tired. There was a thin crust of ice along the bank of the small creek. Hoping he would not have to get his feet wet, he walked along the meandering stream in an easterly direction, looking for a foot log on which to cross. He felt extremely lucky when he found two saplings, one about two feet above the other, leaning across the water. Some storm or strong wind had blessed him by blowing the small trees across the creek to form a natural bridge.

All day he carefully circled around the open areas as he slowly advanced toward Honeywood. Even with the pain from walking on the injured leg, he felt exuberant at the thought of holding Charity in his arms once more. Each painful step was one step closer to the only girl he would ever love, one step closer to the girl he hoped would someday be his wife.

He came to a cluster of tall cedar trees atop an immense Indian mound, and he remembered it as being on the west boundary of Honeywood; he had ridden there a couple of times with Charity. The sight brought a rush of emotion because he knew that he would soon see her. He continued walking faster now, toward paradise. He came to a field road and knew that it led directly to big barns and then to the main house. Another mile and across one more small ridge, and he would be in sight of his destination. The top of the ridge was near. He was almost there. He could see the very tops of the enormous trees that surrounded the house.

He hurried as fast as his legs, and the makeshift crutch, would allow him to go. He reached the top and looked toward the home of his beloved Charity, the place he had so often dreamed of during the long months he had been away. But all he saw were charred remains of the once magnificent trees and ghostly, freestanding chimneys marking massive piles of rubble and ashes where the stately house and regal barns had stood.

He was devastated. At first, he could not imagine what had happened to Charity and her family, and then he had to fight to control his emotions as his imagine began to run rampant. He stood at the crest of the ridge in frozen disbelief and lost track of time. Light was fading when he broke himself out of the spell. With heavy heart, he walked down the road toward the decimated remains of what he remembered as one of the most magnificent homes he had ever seen. He found no one. He walked around and looked for any sign of what might have happened to the proud people who had once nursed him back to health and brightened his life.

Only a couple of the slave houses remained unharmed. It was almost dark when he selected one to shelter him for the night. He had no matches, but he felt his way around the one-room structure until he found a bed. It had a crude frame with ropes stretched from front to back and side to side to support the cornhusk mattress. There was little sleep for him that night, but there was nothing he could do or learn in the darkness, and so he spent a troubled night in the former bed of a slave.

Dawn found him up and out, looking for any sign that might indicate the fate of the McLaurens. His only hope was that they had gone away to live with friends or relatives. He wanted to remain in the area to search for them, but that would make him a deserter, and although there was no more fight left in him, he knew he could not do that. He also wasn't sure he was ready for the truth. He had seen the results of enemy raids on other farms and plantations; many times such raids ended in brutal rape and murder. He would go back to war, but he would return some day. He would stay until he knew the whole story, if it took forever.

CHAPTER 14

Morgan dispiritedly started walking north, back to war. His leg was stiff and sore, but he was able to walk this morning without the aid of the makeshift crutch. As he walked he remembered a neighboring plantation about five miles to the northeast, where he and Charity had ridden one Saturday afternoon. It would be out of his way, but he decided to walk the extra miles in hopes of getting information about Charity and her family. When he came near to what had almost been as grand a plantation as Honeywood, he saw that it too had suffered the same fate as the McLauren's home. He did find a half dozen Negroes around the place, but they were so upset at having lost their homes and livelihood that they could tell him nothing. He resumed his slow, painful walk northward.

About midafternoon he came upon a small, rundown farmhouse, where an old woman sat peeling potatoes on the front porch. "Howdy, ma'am," Morgan greeted her as he entered through the yard gate.

She stared at him a full minute before finally addressing him. "How do, young man. Couldn't make out for a spell which side you was on. Can't see like I used to, and didn't want no Yank coming through that gate. They come here a few weeks ago, musta been a hundred of 'em. Took most everything we had, at least everything they could find. Took our mule, hogs, even our milk cow and her calf. Good thing Paw had some more cows and hogs running loose in the woods. Oh my, ain't I a-goin' on some. You don't want to hear about our troubles. Come on up and rest yourself a spell. You really look tuckered out."

"Thank you, ma'am," Morgan replied as he climbed the steps and took a seat in an old wooden rocking chair. "I am a little tired."

The old woman placed the pan of potatoes on the floor and got up from her chair. "I'll bring you a glass of buttermilk," she said, and before Morgan could reply she disappeared through the front door. In a minute she was back, bringing a large glass full of the cool, white liquid and followed by an old man. "Young man, this here's Paw. Folks round here just call us Maw and Paw Thatcher."

Morgan immediately got to his feet. "I'm Lieutenant Morgan Montgomery, with General Forrest's cavalry. I stopped by to ask if you knew of the whereabouts of the McLaurens of Honeywood Plantation. They are my friends, and their home has been burned."

"Yep, most of the big places 'round here got burnt to the ground," Paw said. "Don't know 'bout your friends. Most of the well-off folks took out when Yanks started all the burnin' and thievin'."

"Young man, come on in the house," Maw said, "and I'll fix you some food."

Morgan started to say that he really couldn't take their food, but Paw anticipated Morgan's reluctance and said, "We got plenty to feed you. The Yankees thought they was cleaning us out, but they didn't. We hid a lot of our stuff before they got here."

"Besides, it's our duty to feed our fightin' boys," Maw added.

Morgan was treated to a meal of fried pork fatback, boiled greens, and a generous hunk of oven-baked cornbread. Even with the haunting thoughts of Charity and her family, he managed to eat the food with a trace of enjoyment. When the old woman insisted that he have a second helping, he said, "Thank you, ma'am, I really can't take any more of your food. Besides, I've really had quite enough. And I must add that it was very good."

"Nonsense," Maw answered. "You don't look like you've had enough to eat in a long time. Like Paw told you, we've got enough to share, and spring is gonna be here soon. Then we'll have even more, with poke and the other wild greens, and soon a garden. So eat up and make us feel proud." Morgan didn't try to rebut her persistence; he just took a second helping and enjoyed both the company and the food.

"Looks like your leg is in bad shape," Paw said when Morgan had finished his second helping of food. "Maw, get him some clean cloth to wrap around that sore. It ain't bleedin', but it sure looks awful."

The old lady went to another room and returned with a large piece of brown cloth. "This was left over from a dress I made," she said. "Don't look like a bandage, but it's clean."

The old man helped Morgan wrap the cloth around his leg several times, outside of his pants, and it was then secured by a firm knot.

Morgan shook the old man's hand and turned toward the old lady. Before he could reach for her hand, she put her arms around him and whispered, "God be with you, young man. We'll pray for you." A short time later the well-fed soldier was again walking north.

Late in the day he came to the camp of a small company of rebel infantry. They shared their meager rations with him and offered him a bedroll. Even though they were strangers to him, he felt a strong sense of kinship among these men who fought side by side for a common cause. He was proud to stay the night with his brothers of the Confederacy. During the usual dialogue around the evening campfire, Morgan told them about Charity and what he had found at Honeywood.

"She is the prettiest and sweetest girls I've ever met. I love her deeply, and I only hope I can find her after this crazy mess is over," he told them.

A sergeant asked him, "Did you talk to anyone around the place? Was there anyone you could ask about your girl and her family?"

"No," Morgan answered, "I could find no one. The plantation was completely deserted. All I found was the terrible waste of a beautiful home and all the buildings except two slave houses. There were no animals and no farm equipment to be seen. I did talk to one old lady who lived a few miles away from the plantation, but she knew nothing at all about them."

One of the older soldiers added his thoughts. "I'll bet they heard about the raiding Yankees and left before they got there. Most likely they went to some safe place where they can stay until the Yankees are gone from around here. Don't worry, son, you'll find your girl after we win this war."

A captain, who had been standing in the shadows nearby and listening, spoke up. "We've been hearing these stories everywhere we go. General Greison and his band of renegades have been methodically pillaging and burning every business, home, church, or farm that was believed to have given aid and comfort to our boys. We know that Grierson has been in central Mississippi during the past two or three weeks."

Morgan's blood ran cold when he thought that Grierson, who had given him his first taste of war back at Edwards Station, was also the one who had devastated Honeywood and the neighboring plantations.

Early the next morning he said good-bye and left the little band, continuing on his trek northward. The next night he managed to "conscript" a horse that was tethered near a Union camp. The horse made traveling a little easier but also more dangerous, because it was much easier to spot a man on horseback than on foot. While walking he could duck behind a tree or dive into tall grass or brush at the first sign of danger.

Twice he came close to being captured or killed by the enemy. On one occasion he was eating with a farm family when a Yankee patrol rode into the front yard. Morgan ran out the back door and across a short distance to the barn where his horse was being fed by the young son of the farmer. Keeping the barn between himself and the house, he quickly led the horse into a nearby patch of woods, where he mounted and made his escape without the patrol even knowing he had been there.

Another time he rode into the middle of a Union picket line before he realized they were there. It was nearly dark, and he was trying to locate a suitable place to bed down for the night when one of the pickets yelled a challenge, "Who goes there, friend or foe?" Morgan recognized the curt Yankee brogue, and without hesitation he turned his mount and sent the animal racing back down the road. He was amazed at not hearing musket fire from the pickets.

After two weeks of looking, dodging, hiding out, and going hungry and cold, he located his regiment. He was about ready to give up the search and join whatever unit he came across, when he came upon five rebels standing picket duty. "Halt where you are," one of them commended. I see your uniform, but who are you?"

"I'm Lieutenant Morgan Montgomery. I'm looking for General Forrest's Command."

"Well, maybe you've found it, and maybe you haven't," another man said. "You look dirty and ragged like most Rebs these days, but maybe you could tell us what you're doing on a Yankee horse and saddle."

Morgan was exuberant over the possibility that he had found his unit, but he was bone tired and weary and didn't want to be delayed or to answer a lot of questions. "I've been separated from my unit for two or three weeks, I'm not sure of how long. As for the hoarse and saddle, I borrowed them from a Yankee. Just tell me whether or not I'm near Forrest's camp."

The man who had first challenged him answered, "The camp is spread out all along the road, starting about a half mile that way, so go ahead on." He pointed down the road.

Morgan replied, "Thank you, men, and good day," as he rode away. He stopped as he came across the first group of soldiers and asked directions to find General Forrest.

He reported directly to Forrest, ashamed that he had failed in his mission to return with the twelve guns. He gave a full report to the general and was surprised when Forrest congratulated him on a job well done. "It was just about as important to deprive the Yankees of their use as it was to bring 'em back to me. I reckon you've done exactly what I'da done in the same place."

Morgan's leg was not healing very fast, and so he had one of the surgeons look at it. "Young man," the old doctor said as he cleaned and bandaged the infected wound, "I understand you've been traveling on this leg for two weeks, but I don't see how you've kept going. I'm ordering you to stay off it as much as possible for at least another week, and try to get plenty of rest. I believe it's gonna heal very well, but only if you give it some help."

As Morgan enjoyed his first leisurely camp meal in weeks, he began to realize just how exhausted he really was. When he had finished eating, he made down a bed in one of the officers' tents and slept for eighteen hours.

There was a letter waiting for him when he awoke. It was from Martha Newton. He had received many letters, but this was the first one from home in more than six months. The news was not good.

Dearest Morgan,

First, let me say that we miss you so very much. You are constantly on our minds and in our hearts and in our prayers. We have not received a letter from you in several months, but I do understand about the mail.

It is with much sadness in my heart that I tell you the news. John is seriously ill and is no longer able to get out of bed. He was the victim of enemy hostility and is not recovering well.

Most of the Negroes have been conscripted by the Union soldiers. Caleb and Rufus were forced to join the Union Army. Then Sissy was taken away. Only one old man remains with us. But we are getting by.

Sam Watkins has been home for a few days while recuperating from a wound he received in a battle near Chattanooga.

Sincerely,
Martha Newton

During Morgan's absence, Forrest had reorganized his forces into four brigades, commanded by General R. V. Richardson and Colonels Tyree Bell, Robert McCullock, and Jeffrey Forrest, the general's younger brother. Morgan was assigned to McCullock's brigade and, to his surprise, promoted to the rank of captain.

The war now took on a new meaning for Morgan. For months after his enlistment, the war had been something exciting, an adventure—often brutal and unpleasant, but an adventure nonetheless. Now more than ever, he felt a real calling to fight and prevail. His cause was no longer a mere expression of words, spoken on behalf of a way of life or one's country. His cause had been heightened by the ever-present perception that much that he had loved may have been lost forever. He felt that he would never be allowed to go back to his former life with the Newtons, and deep within the recesses of his mind, he believed that Charity might also be lost to him forever. Now he had to do anything within his power to stop those responsible for all the destruction and devastation against the citizens of the South. He threw himself into the war effort with total dedication and a reckless disregard for personal safety.

In early March 1864, General Forrest took his forces north to raid in west Tennessee and Kentucky. But he left General McCullock's brigade behind to protect the citizens of the area against the many small units of the enemy, and the loosely organized bands of marauding deserters who were stealing horses and supplies and generally harassing the civilian population. McCullock also had orders to engage General Grierson's cavalry at every opportunity. Morgan would have preferred to go with Forrest, but he accepted the orders and said nothing. However, after thinking things over, he decided that there was a bright side to staying behind. He might get the opportunity to learn something of the events that brought about the destruction of Honeywood and the disappearance of the McLaurens.

The next few weeks were generally uneventful. A few deserters were caught, and there were half a dozen skirmishes with enemy patrols and scouting parties, but nothing major happened. Morgan requested to take a small patrol into the area around Raymond. McCullock granted permission to take twenty men, telling Morgan that he would be giving his men and animals a rest period for a few days and would not be moving from the present campsite.

The patrol rode into Raymond on Sunday morning, and Morgan allowed his men to attend service at one of the three local churches, if they wished to. He attended service at the church where the McLaurens had taken him during the later days of his recuperation.

Very few people were at the service, not nearly as many as when he worshiped there before. The ones attending were mostly old men, women, and small children.

The preacher gave a short sermon but prayed a very long prayer. He prayed for the men in the war, for those left behind, and for the fighting to soon end. Being there seemed to strengthen Morgan's faith, but it also made his sad as he remembered those wonderful days when he was there with Charity.

After the service he asked the preacher and some of the members of the congregation if they knew anything about the McLaurens, but no one did. He talked to several citizens around town that afternoon, with the same results.

He was about ready to call his men together to leave when he saw an old Negro man ambling down a side street near where the horses were hitched. There was something familiar about the old man. Could it be? It was old Moses, the man who had driven the wagon when Morgan was taken to the McLauren home from the hospital, the man who had helped take care of him during those terrible near-death days of feverish nightmares and delusions.

"Moses!" Morgan called out. The old man crouched a little lower and ducked around the corner of a building, but Morgan ran after him. When he rounded the corner, he saw the old man again only a few feet away. "Moses," he called out again. The old man attempted to shuffle a little faster. "Moses, it's me, Morgan Montgomery."

The old man stopped in his tracks and slowly turned to face Morgan. For a moment he stood silent like a weather-beaten statue as his eyes gazed on Morgan. Then a smile slowly appeared on his face.

"Lawdy, it sho is you. I never did think these ole eyes would ever see you again."

Morgan ran to the old man and embraced him. "I was beginning to think I would never find anyone from Honeywood again," he told

Moses. "I've been trying to find someone who could tell me what happened. Can you tell me what took place out there, and where the McLaurens went?"

"Well, Masser Morgan, I can tell you some 'bout what happen to us all, but I can't tell ye zackly where de Masser done took his famly."

They were in front of an abandoned store building. Morgan noticed a long wooden bench that had been left in front of the old building. He took Moses by the arm as he said, "Let's rest over there while we talk. I want to hear everything."

After the two men were comfortably seated, Moses told his story, and Morgan was able to get a clear picture of what of what had taken place. Moses told of how a hundred or more Union horsemen came to Honeywood late one afternoon. Albert got word that they were coming just before they arrived and sent Charity and Mrs. McLauren to one of the slave houses to hide. The leader of the soldiers first demanded food for his men and their horses. Later they went through the house and the barns, taking whatever they wanted. When Albert protested to the commanding officer, the man hit him across the head with the flat side of his saber, knocking him to the ground, bleeding and unconscious. Mrs. McLauren saw what happened and came running from her hiding place. Two men caught her before she ever got near the officer who had hit Albert. They dragged her into one of the barns, and Moses heard her scream. Several of the slaves started toward the barn, but other soldiers held guns on them, telling them that it was white men's business and to stay away from the barn. Moses said that he then slipped to the house where Charity was hiding. He threw a quilt over her head and slipped her out the back way, across a field of corn stalks, and into a small grove of woods. Just as it was getting dark, they saw fire coming from the main house. Later there were several large fires burning at the same time, lighting up the countryside with an eerie red glow.

The next morning Moses convinced Charity to stay in hiding while he went back to see if anyone or anything was left. He got close to the smoldering ruins to see that the Yankee invaders had gone. He returned to the woods and brought Charity out with him. As they got near to what had been their home, they saw all the smoke and destruction, and Charity started to weep. They located Albert and Mrs. McLauren in the rose gazebo, which appeared to be the only structure around that had been left undamaged, other than two small slave houses. Albert and his wife were being attended by Sudie and several other black women. Both of the McLaurens looked bad, and Mrs. McLauren couldn't stop crying.

All the young adult slaves had been taken away, but the older men set about to build temporary shelter out of whatever scraps they could find. The McLaurens were moved into one of the small houses. Young Charles McLauren had been taken away by the raiders, but the next night he and two of the young slaves ran away from their captors and returned to the plantation.

By removing good parts from several damaged wagons, Albert managed to construct three good wagons. A few days later, with the few things they were able to salvage, the four McLaurens, along with Sudie and Claude, drove away from what had been their home. All the slaves who were still there had been handed papers by Thomas, giving them their freedom. He told them they could stay there as long as they wanted, and that they could have anything they could recover from the plantation. Moses ended his story by saying, "I don't member exactly what Masser Albert say, but it was something about Texas."

*   *   *

It was well after noon before Morgan and his men rode out of the little town. They were a full day's ride from McCullom's bivouac, and so late in the afternoon Morgan started looking for a suitable place to camp for the night. There were at least two hours of daylight left, but he preferred to pick a good location early, rather than take a chance on finding a safe place nearer dark. They came to a small stream with a patch of woods that would provide good concealment. Morgan ordered his men to dismount and make camp. They had just settled in for cold rations and rest when a young soldier, called Buckshot, came to Morgan and said that his horse had strayed away, and he was going to look for it. It was almost an hour later when Buckshot returned, riding hard. "Yankees!" he yelled as he rode into camp. "They were saddlin' up a few minutes ago, so they will be here soon."

"Where were they?" Morgan asked. "How far away?"

"They're camped up the road, no more'n two miles north of here. I found my horse and was leadin' him back to camp when I saw this Yankee. He was watchin' our camp. I only had my pistol, and he was too far away to hit with that thing. He mounted up and eased his horse away, real quiet like, so I followed him. I got close enough to see him report to someone, probably an officer. That was when they started saddlin' their horses, and so I cut a trail back here. I 'spect they'll be here in a few minutes."

"How many were there?" Morgan asked.

"I'd say about thirty, maybe even forty, but no more'n that," Buckshot answered.

"Men, collect some wood for a fire, and do it quick." Morgan ordered. "Make sure some of the wood is green, so it'll smoke a lot."

In less than two minutes, some of the men collected small twigs and had them blazing. Others quickly piled on larger sticks. As soon as he was sure that the fire would burn well, Morgan ordered, "Leave everything here but your carbines and pistols, and follow me."

Staying off the road and keeping a sharp eye out for any activity in the direction from which he expected the Yankees to come, he led his men about five hundred yards north of camp. He ordered them to take up positions in the tall grass and wait for his order to fire. They didn't have to wait long. The blue-coated riders came down the road, first at a slow trot and then picking up speed as they came nearer. When they were no more than two hundred yards from Morgan and his men, a Yankee officer drew his saber, waved it over his head and yelled, "Charge!" The air was instantly filled with exuberant shouts and yells as Yankee riders prodded their horses into full gallop, toward what they thought was an unsuspecting rebel camp.

"Fire!" Morgan yelled

Twenty-one carbines discharged in unison, followed by rapid fire from twenty-one pistols. Thirty-six horses galloped by with empty saddles. Morgan felt a wave of sick remorse as thirty-six bodies paved the road, blue and red. This was war, and he had killed before, several times, but he had never felt more alone than he did at that moment. Although those dead men had been trying to kill him and his men, he had given the order, a single word that snuffed out so many lives. *God, forgive me, forgive us all on both sides, because this can't be right.*

CHAPTER 15

During the following year, Morgan participated in the battles of Brice's Cross Roads, Tupelo, Pulaski, Johnsonville, Spring Hill, Franklin, and Selma. On April 2, 1865, during the battle of Selma, he was critically wounded. It happened when his horse was killed under him during the heat of battle. The dying animal fell on his leg, and he was unable to free himself. A Union soldier took advantage of his defenseless condition and stuck him through the back with a bayonet.

This was another new experience for Morgan, being in the hands of the enemy. He was in a Union hospital and being well cared for, but he was still a prisoner of war.

There had first been some rough treatment when he was taken by Union soldiers during battle. When they saw that he was seriously wounded, they were a little more gentle with him. He was loaded into a wagon with two wounded Union soldiers and transported to a field hospital. During the trip he passed out from loss of blood. When he came to he was in a large tent with several other patients. He tried to get off the small cot but hardly had the strength to raise his head. Two days later he was moved to a hospital in a large private home that had been commandeered by the Union Army.

It was while recovering from his wound in the Union hospital that he learned that the fighting was all over. Generals Grant and Lee had met in a house owned by a Southern farmer named Wilmer

McLane, in the little country community of Appomattox Court House, Virginia, and signed the articles of surrender. The South would pay a drastic price for having dared to defend a way of life. Abraham Lincoln called for "Malice toward none ... charity for all," hoping to heal the nation's wounds. But the president's words went unheeded by those who took power after his assassination.

On the first day of June 1865, Morgan was released from the Union hospital and paroled. He was pleasantly surprised when the hospital commander handed him more than a hundred dollars in gold. It was money Morgan had saved from his paltry military pay throughout his entire enlistment in the Confederate army. He had carried it in a money belt under his clothes, and the surgeons discovered it while treating his wound.

He considered going directly to Texas to search for Charity, but knowing that such a search might take him far and wide, he would first go home to Columbia, Tennessee, to see the Newtons. It had been more than a year since he had heard from them. He didn't have the strength to walk very far, but thanks to the Union commander's honest act, he had money to ride a train. Learning that the nearest passenger station was in Montgomery, he managed to get a ride on a freight wagon from the Union supply depot at Selma to the outskirts of Montgomery. He then walked the distance of two miles to the railroad station. He found the station to be a beehive of activity and had to wait three days to get on a train, where the only thing available to a former rebel officer was an open freight car. Even for that he had to pay, but the fare was only six dollars to ride all the way to Nashville, much less than a ticket on a passenger coach.

In Nashville he was told there would be no train to Columbia for several days, and even then he could not be promised passage. Extremely anxious to get back to Columbia and Oakmont, he purchased a horse and saddle with seventy dollars of his savings. His trip to Nashville had cost him about ten dollars for train fare and food, which left him with a little over twenty dollars, but that would be quite enough to get home.

The first night out of Nashville, he stayed at a small wayside inn near Franklin. With breakfast before daylight, sunup found him well on his way toward Columbia. During the two-day ride, he thought much about his future. He would visit with the Newtons long enough to make sure that everything was well with them, and then he would travel to Texas and find Charity. After making her his wife, he would return to Oakmont and work hard to make it a successful plantation again.

It could be done without slave labor. He hoped that many of the former slaves would return to work. He would try to find every one of them and offer them a paying job. If that did not work out, he would hire good workers, white or black, and make Oakmont an even more prosperous place than it had been before the war. And he would insist that John and Martha Newton do some traveling, maybe to Europe. It was fitting that they now enjoy the fruits of their many years of labor. Yes, he and Charity would take care of the Newtons and make sure they lived the rest of their lives in comfort.

However, the very first thing on his agenda was to ask Sissy to cook him the grandest meal she had ever prepared. Food would probably be in short supply, but Sissy could work magic with anything available. All the many hungry times he had spent dreaming of the scrumptious food her artistic hands could prepare, and now, in a matter of hours, he would be able to put his feet under Martha Newton's dining table and partake of the products of Sissy's culinary skills. What about Caleb and Rufus? Would they come back? Martha Newton's letter said that the Yankees had taken them away, but they would surely come back home after the war. It would be so good to have everyone back together again. It would take some time, but maybe when things were put back to normal again, he could start forgetting some of the horrible things he had witnessed, and even participated in, during the past years.

The horse Morgan had purchased in Nashville was a good mount, a high-stepping walker, and he made excellent time. By mid-afternoon of the second day, he came to the outskirts of Columbia, but things didn't look the same. He saw standing chimneys and rubble where fine homes had stood. The once productive farmland looked as if it had not been worked in years. Fences were in disrepair, and the fields had grown over in weeds and bushes. And everywhere there was a noticeable absence of livestock.

As he rode into town, he found many of the familiar homes either in shambles or completely missing from what had once been well-landscaped lawns. The streets had not been maintained, and there were large holes and deep ruts everywhere. There had always been pleasant greetings from everyone he met, but now the friendly atmosphere was missing. The few people on the streets appeared lethargic and unfriendly.

As he rode past Mayes Hardware Store, Jennie Mayes came running out of the front door of the establishment. "Morgan! Oh, Morgan! Is it really you?"

Surprised and happy to see a smiling face, Morgan quickly dismounted and stepped to meet her. "Hello, Jennie. Yes, it's me." He intended to offer her his hand, but instead she put her arms around his neck and gave him a friendly hug, right in the middle of Garden Street.

"Morgan, I'm so glad to see you. We heard you were dead. So many of our boys didn't come back, you know. Wait until Sam hears that you're back. He's down in Mount Pleasant today, taking care of some family business."

"How is Sam? I mean, did he come through the war all right? I know he was wounded a couple of times."

"He's just fine. He should be back in town later this afternoon. Why don't you come to our house for supper tonight? Sam will be there, and you two can catch up on all your war talk."

"Jennie, I'd love to be with you and Sam tonight, but I want to spend the time with Martha and John, and I've been thinking about Sissy's cooking all day. But I do hope we three can get together soon. It'll be like old times."

The pleasant smile faded from Jennie's face, and tears began to well in her eyes. "Oh, Morgan, you don't know. Forgive me."

"Know what, Jennie?"

"Then you haven't been home, have you?"

"No, I haven't been home. I was on my way there when I saw you. You're the very first person I've talked to in Columbia. But what don't I know? What are you talking about?"

"Please, come inside with me, Morgan. I'd like for you to talk to my father."

Troubled over what Jennie might be trying to tell him, Morgan hitched his horse at the hitch rail and followed her into the store. Mr. Mayes stood behind a long counter going through a stack of papers when Morgan and Jennie approached. "Daddy, look who's back. It's Morgan Montgomery. And Daddy, he's not been home. He doesn't know about anything that's happened around here, so I want you to talk to him."

"Hello, Morgan, it's good to see you back," the older man said, and he extended his hand.

"Hello, Mister Mayes. It's good to be back," Morgan replied as he shook the older man's hand.

"Young man," John Mayes said, and then paused as if he were looking for the right words. "When did you last hear from John and Martha?"

"It's been over a year, and that letter was several months old," Morgan answered.

"Morgan, I'm afraid I must be the bearer of some exceedingly bad news. John and Martha Newton are no longer with us. They've both been called to their heavenly home. John passed on about a year ago, and we buried Martha only a few weeks ago."

Because he was only partially recovered from the near fatal wound, and was weak from the long stay in the Union hospital, the shock of such news overpowered Morgan. He felt his legs giving way under him, and everything went black. The next thing he remembered was the spirited aroma of smelling salts.

"Morgan, can you hear me? Are you all right? Morgan, please wake up."

"Charity, is that you? Oh, Charity, I've found you," Morgan heard a distant voice saying.

"No, Morgan, it's me, Jennie Mayes; don't you remember?"

As awareness returned, he knew that he had been hearing his own voice. He changed from a state of confusion to one of embarrassment. "I'm sorry, Jennie. For a moment I thought you were someone I knew during the war."

"No need to apologize, Morgan. But you simply must tell me all about this Charity."

"Jennie, get the buggy and take Morgan to our house," John Mayes told his daughter. "After he's rested and had supper with us, I'll tell him the rest of the story." Turning to Morgan, he said, "I'll have a boy from the stables tend to your horse and put it up for the night. It will be fresh in the morning if you need it."

Jennie drove Morgan to the Mayes home on Sixth Street, and the maid showed him to a guest bedroom. He quickly fell asleep on the high poster bed. It was getting dark when he awoke to a knock at the door. He invited the person who had knocked to come in. The door was opened by an elderly black man who gave a pleasant smile as he said, "Mister Morgan, the Mayes will have supper in an hour.

I hope you don't mind, but I took the liberty of having a hot bath brought up for you, and a razor and change of clothes."

To Morgan's pleasant surprise, in the center of the room was a large brass bathtub filled with warm water, which had been brought up earlier while he was asleep. There was also a nice suit of clothes draped across the footboard of the bed. The old man left after Morgan thanked him for the bath and clothes. The water in the tub was still pleasantly warm. Thirty minutes later, rested, bathed, shaved, and in a clean suit of clothes, Morgan walked down the long, winding staircase to be greeted by Mr. Mayes and Sam Watkins, his boyhood friend and hunting companion.

Mr. Mayes soon excused himself to attend to something. Morgan and Sam spent the next thirty minutes talking about old times and the future, but deliberately avoiding the subject of the war. Sam had taken a position with Mayes Mercantile Co. until he decided on a business of his own, and he and Jennie would be married in a few months. Morgan was happy to see Sam, but he really didn't feel like talking about his future. He only told his old friend that he had made a few plans. He was glad when they were called to dinner.

When the meal was over, Mr. Mayes invited Morgan to join him on the veranda. They sat in large wicker chairs with thick cushions and remained quiet for several minutes. Morgan waited for his host to speak, and Mr. Mayes seemed to be trying to think of the right thing to say. Finally, the older man broke the silence. "Well, Morgan, I'm sure you would like to know what happened around here, and especially what took place at Oakmont."

To which Morgan replied, "Yes, sir, I would like to hear everything."

Mr. Mayes took a pipe out of his coat pocket and filled it with tobacco from a leather pouch. He lit it with a match, and took a few puffs before starting. "Shortly after you enlisted, the first band of raiding Yankees came through. They took most of the food that hadn't been hidden well enough, and most of the cattle and horses. John Newton didn't like it, none of us did, but there was nothing we could do. Our store was almost cleaned out, without a sign of payment for anything. Things went from bad to worse. What the Yankees didn't get, the Southern boys later took.

"About a year and a half ago, a Union regiment came through, demanding more food and supplies. There was none to give. Their commanding officer took a raiding party out to Oakmont and told John Newton that he was freeing his slaves, although John had already set them all free. They took those two boys you and Sam used to hunt and fish with—what were their names?"

"Caleb and Rufus."

"Yes, Caleb and Rufus. John told me later that the boys didn't want to go at all; in fact, none of them wanted to go. It seems that John didn't say very much until they took Sissy kicking and screaming. John became very angry and demanded that the soldiers keep their hands off his people. Two of the raiders held John while two or three others took turns beating him. John never recovered from the attack. Doctor Prichert said that he suffered brain damage. He was never able to get out of bed, and he died some three months later. Martha tried to hang on, but with no help she had a very rough time of it.

"Then, as soon as the war was over, we became inundated with Northern carpetbaggers. They had the authority to take over the courthouse and all the county records. They declared that most of the better farms and plantations around here were behind on tax payments. They accused the Newtons of being ten years behind on their taxes. We all knew it wasn't true, but we had no way to prove it, not having access to the records. Several of us made up enough money to pay the so-called back taxes for Martha, but we were told that the property had already been sold for the tax money. Martha was put off the property with only her clothes and a few items of personal property. She moved in with friends, but she passed a few weeks ago. Old Doc Prichert says that he thinks the real cause of death was a broken heart."

Mr. Mayes stopped talking at that point. It was a warm June night, and the sounds of insects could be heard in any direction as both men remained silent for a long time.

Morgan finally broke the silence. "Is there anything that can be done? There has to be some way to punish the people who commit such grievous acts against kind and gentle people like the Newtons."

"Morgan, we lost the war, and we're now completely at their mercy. The carpetbaggers are in total control, and they change the law almost daily, as it serves their needs. They have taken over the state and local government, and they'll own anything and everything of value before it's over."

"It sounds worse than what was done during the war," Morgan said. "Then, the stealing and pillaging was mostly for food and supplies, not for personal gain and profit. I can't just stand by and let them get away with what they've done to those wonderful people."

"My boy, there's not a single thing you can do. You'll only get yourself into serious trouble if you even think about trying anything. I don't know if you ever knew Thomas Potter, who farmed land along the banks of Duck River. He tried to keep one of the carpetbaggers off his land with a gun. They burned his house, took him prisoner, tried him a week later, and immediately hanged him. We've had several people try to stand up for their rights, only to end up stretching rope. I know how you must feel, but for your sake and for the sake of your friends, please don't try anything."

The next morning Morgan rode out to visit the graves of John and Martha Newton, the two people whose unselfish love and kindness had forever changed the life of a young orphan boy from Lewis County. After an hour he said his final good-bye and returned to town. Later that morning he purchased a bedroll and a week's supply of food for himself and his horse, said farewell to old friends, and set out for Memphis. Both Sam Watkins and Mr. Mayes tried to give him money, but he convinced them both that he had enough to get him to Memphis. He never told them that he planned to go all the way to Texas.

Each night of his trek to Memphis he camped out and felt perfectly comfortable doing so. He had been sleeping on the ground almost every night for nearly three years. He arrived in Memphis on the morning of his seventh day and immediately looked for the home of General Nathan Bedford Forrest. The town reminded Morgan of an anthill, working with horse-drawn vehicles of every description and riders on horseback, all mixing and mingling with countless pedestrians.

He approached a policeman who was standing on a street corner and asked, "Pardon me, Officer, can you tell me where Mister Bedford Forrest lives?"

The policeman thought for a moment and replied, "No, sir, I'm afraid I can't help you. I know he lives around here someplace, but I don't know exactly where."

Morgan thanked the officer and walked on. Next, he entered a barber shop and asked one of the barbers the same question. The barber replied, "I don't know where he lives, but he has an office just a few blocks from here." He proceeded to describe the building and give directions to the office.

Upon arriving at the office, Morgan was told that Forrest had just left for dinner at a hotel a few doors down the street. Being very hungry from only having trail food for a week, Morgan decided to go to the same place to eat. As he entered the lobby and was about to ask directions to the dining room, he saw Forrest. His former leader was engaged in conversation with two other men.

Forrest noticed him approaching and immediately turned away from the men he had been talking with, almost running to Morgan. "Morgan Montgomery! As I live and breathe, it's really you. I received a report that you were killed at Selma. But I can see that the report was less than accurate. How are you, my boy?"

Morgan returned a hearty handshake and replied, "I'm doing very well, sir, and how are you?"

"Oh, I'm doin' fine for an old war horse. I was about to put on the feed bag, so you'll eat with me, and that's an order," Forrest said, followed by a little laugh.

"Sir, I'd be delighted."

"Come on over here and meet some people." Morgan followed him over to where the two men were waiting. "Gentlemen, I'd like for you to meet one of the finest young cavalry officers to ever serve under me. This is Morgan Montgomery. Morgan, meet James Miller and Richard Dunkin. Gentlemen, let's have some good food while we talk."

After they were seated in the large dining room, Forrest said, "Morgan, these gentlemen are my new partners in a Mississippi farming venture. I own a few thousand acres just a few miles across the state line, and they've agreed to help me run a farming operation there."

Food was ordered and served, and for a few minutes nothing was said but a few trivial comments. Then Forrest asked, "What about John and Martha? How're they gettin' along?"

"Sir, they've passed away."

"What! You don't mean it." Forrest paused and then said, "My God, Morgan, this is really sad news. Can you tell me what happened to them? Did it have to do with the war?"

Morgan proceeded to tell the story as Mr. Mayes had told it to him. Then James Miller replied, "It's sad that some of our people have to act like that. We didn't fight a war to end up treating people like that."

Then Forrest said to Morgan, "I'm afraid I failed to tell you that these gentlemen were on the Union side. You might think it's a little strange that I decided to hook up with my former enemies, but they're good men. There were good men on both sides, and the sooner we recognize that fact and put the war behind us, the better for everyone. That's what I'm trying hard to do, and so are these gentlemen."

Morgan had learned that Forrest was a reasonable and level-headed man during the time he served under him, and he wasn't really surprised that his former commander had taken these men as partners. He hoped that everyone, from both sides, would act the same.

Forrest and his two new partners talked farming business as they finished their meal. Soon Miller and Dunkin excused themselves and left the dining room. "Well, Morgan, what you got planned for your future?"

Morgan told him about the disappearance of Charity and her family, and how he planned to go to Texas to find them. "I'd sure like to have you as my guest for a spell, but if you really want to go to Texas, there's a riverboat down at the docks that'll be leavin' for New Orleans in a couple of hours. I'm sure I can get you passage, if you want me to. You might have to sleep on deck, but that won't be new to you. I don't think there'll be another one in two weeks."

"I'd like very much to go on the one today; the sooner the better."

"If I may ask, what's your financial situation? You got plenty of money for boat fare?"

"I don't have, but I plan to sell my horse and saddle. It's a good Tennessee walker, and it should bring enough for passage to New Orleans and on to Galveston."

"Let's go take a look at this walkin' horse. I might be interested. Where you got the animal now?"

"I left it hitched in front of your office."

As they walked back to the office, Forrest explained why he had taken on the former Union officers as partners. "They can get things that are not available to me, such as money to hire hands and purchase seed and supplies. Being Unionists, they won't have to go through all the government paperwork that I'd have to put up with. They were both good farmers in Ohio before the war, and we all agree that they will do better down here, considering the better climate and good soil. I have plenty of land, and the truth is, I plan to take on others like them if I can find the right people. I'll make a place for you, if you ever come back this way again."

Morgan enjoyed the walk, even though the sidewalk was crowded and noisy. The past days in the saddle made him appreciate a little walking. Forrest looked Morgan's horse over and said, "Morgan, I'll give you two hundred dollars for the horse and saddle. There aren't many good horses left around here. Most of what you can find have been ruined by one of the armies or the other, starved and rode too hard."

Morgan thought that two hundred dollars was too much, but he decided not to say anything because he knew that Forrest was trying to help him out. Forrest wrote a quick letter and sent it out with an office boy. The boy was back in thirty minutes with a reply. "Morgan, you're booked on the New Orleans boat, but we'd better get you on down there. They'll be leaving soon; it was supposed to have been at noon, but I was told that they are running a little late." He turned to the same office boy and said, "Go around the livery stable and get my carriage, and tell them to make it snappy."

They were soon heading for the docks as Forrest maneuvered the team through heavy traffic. At the dock Forrest gave Morgan a manly hug and said, "Good luck in finding your lady, and God go with you. And let me hear from you. Just send a letter to general delivery, Memphis, and I'll get it."

Chapter 16

Although Forrest had rushed to get Morgan to the dock for a twelve o'clock departure, it was near two o'clock when the boat actually left Memphis. When Morgan went aboard, he was told that he only had deck passage, which meant he would have no place to sleep other than on the deck. He also learned that food would only be served to those who purchased tickets for a stateroom or berth. He had not counted on that and had not brought food for the trip. One of the deck hands later told him that they would be stopping at several towns along the river, and he would be able to get food in one of several dock-side eating establishments.

It was almost nine o'clock when three long blasts from the boat's shrill whistle sounded, announcing their arrival at Helena, Arkansas. Morgan asked one of the hands if he would be able to get food there and was told that everything was closed for the night. A kind old gentleman who also had only deck passage overheard what Morgan had been told. He opened his valise, pulled out a parcel wrapped in brown paper, and opened it to expose a large loaf of brown bread, which was already sliced. He handed a thick slice to Morgan and said, "Here, young man, eat this. It's not fancy, but it's filling."

Morgan was about to tall him no, but the old man insisted before he could get his words out. "I've got plenty, and I'm only going to Greenville. We'll be there before I could eat all of this." Morgan thanked the gentleman and enjoyed the gift.

The boat remained at dockside until dawn the next morning. Morgan overheard a deckhand tell someone that the river was too dangerous to travel at night. The hand said that they had traveled into the night getting there, but only because they had been late departing Memphis.

The night was cool, and Morgan was comfortable with his blanket pulled over him, which also kept out the flying insects. The wooden deck boards were much harder than the ground on which he was used to sleeping, and he had some difficulty falling asleep. He was surprised, however, when he awoke at dawn after sleeping through the night. He got up and secured his bedroll while the deckhands were busy casting off for the continued trip down river. There was a long blast from the whistle, and they were again on their way.

Morgan knew very little about riverboats, but he liked talking to the crew members, especially a very friendly one named Robert, when their time permitted, and he learned a lot about steamboats from them. The boat on which he was traveling was a steam-powered side-wheeler with two high, red smoke stacks. It carried freight and passengers between Memphis and New Orleans, making the trip every nine days.

Although Morgan was apprehensive about his search for Charity and his future in general, the boat ride became very pleasant for him. The gentle motion of the boat, the sound of the rushing water as the bow cut its way down stream, and the melodic waterfall sounds made by the twin side-wheels as they pushed the boat forward—all helped him to relax and clear his mind.

As night approached, the captain steered the boat into a large, deepwater cove. There was a ding, ding, ding of the boat's bell, the side-wheels reversed, and the boat came to a stop. Two small boats were put into the water, and three deck hands in each boat rowed to opposite banks, each pulling a large mooring rope. The ropes were then tied to trees, securing the large boat for the night. Robert, the deckhand, came around and engaged Morgan in conversation. "It'll take us about two hours to get to Greenville in the morning. We usually get there the second night out, but there's recently been some heavy rains that washed a lot of debris into the river, and the captain has to go slower." He handed Morgan a large ham sandwich wrapped in paper. "It's from the galley. It was part of my meal, but there was a lot more than I wanted. Anyway, the captain don't mind, seeing as how we are running late." He followed up by saying, "They don't pay much, but they sure feed us well."

The boat whistle woke Morgan before sunup the nest morning, and they were on their way, arriving at the Greenville landing a little more than two hours later. Passengers were told they would only be there two hours for cargo to be loaded. The gangplank was put out and Morgan went ashore. He spotted a sign along the waterfront with only two words, "Eat Here." The building was small and weather-beaten, but the food was delicious. He had three eggs, a large steak, and four biscuits with a thick slab of butter and homemade jam.

When he paid for his food, he asked the man where he could find a place to buy food for a trip. He was told where he would find a general store less then a block away. He found the store and purchased enough food for the remainder of the voyage.

The next portion of the trip was pleasant and uneventful. They arrived in Vicksburg before nightfall, and deckhands moored the boat at the landing near two other boats. Morgan elected not to go ashore; he had heard about all of the war damage and he didn't wish to see the reminders.

They arrived in Natchez well before dark the next day, and the crew informed the passengers that they would depart at dawn the next morning. Robert told Morgan that the section of Natchez along the waterfront was known as "Natchez under the hill" because a high bluff separated it from the rest of the town. "If you're going ashore, it'll be best that you not hang around down there. It's a rowdy place, lots of fights and even killings. If you want to eat, you'd best go up on the hill; lots of good eating placer up there."

Morgan took his advice and followed the steep road to the top of the hill and to the beautiful old town. After he had eaten a good meal, he decided to look around before going back down to the boat. He was impressed with all the old buildings that appeared to have escaped the ravages of war.

The next morning several new people boarded the boat for the trip down river. In talking to a gentleman from Natchez, Morgan learned that the town had surrendered early on in the war, thus avoiding much of the fighting and destruction suffered by other southern towns.

During the day they met several other boats heading north, and occasionally another southbound boat could be seen around a bend ahead of them. When they arrived in Baton Rouge, the docks were crowded with other boats. Morgan still had plenty of the food that he had purchased in Greenville, and so he decided not to go ashore to eat. His body benefited from the rest and felt rejuvenated from all the war wounds.

The river traffic was heavy the next day. The trip had become a little less interesting after Natchez, and Morgan was glad when they arrived in New Orleans.

Morgan had enjoyed the boat ride, partly because it hade given him a lot of time to think about his future. He might never go back to Tennessee, and he was sure he would never fight in another war, but he would do everything in his power to find Charity. That was all he wanted from life—to see Charity again, to hold her hand, to walk with her, to kiss her lips, and to make her his wife. If God would grant him that, he would be forever thankful and forever happy.

*   *   *

New Orleans moved at a much slower pace than Memphis, or so it seemed to Morgan, as he looked for an inexpensive room. He would have to be thrifty with his money so as not to run out before he got to Texas. The boat fare from Memphis had been nearly thirty dollars. He had prepaid sixty dollars for passage on a steamer bound for Galveston, Texas, but it would not depart for two days. There was now a little over a hundred dollars in his money belt, and he had no way of knowing how long that would have to last him.

He found a rooming house where he could eat and sleep for three dollars a day. It was one of the large, rundown houses near the waterfront, frequented mostly by sailors and longshoremen. It wasn't what he preferred, but it would have to do. He was assigned to a room with three small beds but was told that the other beds were not taken.

He passed the time during his wait in New Orleans by exploring the many diverse sections of the old city. He visited the market place, many of the small shops near the docks, the magnificently appointed streets of some of the beautiful old residential sections. He could enjoy living in such a splendid city—but that was not his destiny.

The night before he was to board the boat for Galveston, he was very tired from all the walking and slept soundly. He awoke before daybreak with the notion that something was wrong. He lit an oil lamp and saw that the other two beds were still not occupied. Checking his bedroll, which served as his only luggage, he found nothing out of place. Deciding to sleep a little longer, he blew out the small flame in the lamp and went back to his bed. He was almost asleep when it dawned on him: his money belt was missing. How could it have happened? It had been safely fastened around his waist, or so he thought. Relighting the lamp, he looked around the room, but it was no use. Someone had entered the room during his sound sleep and skillfully removed the money belt. And he knew he could do nothing.

Fortunately, he had paid for his passage in advance. He was now completely without funds, other than a couple of dollars in small change in his pocket, but he would be able to get to Texas.

At the appointed time he went aboard the boat. He found the captain and explained his circumstances, asking if he could work for his food during the three-day trip. The captain gladly obliged, and Morgan worked in the galley. He had never dreamed he would be doing such work as peeling potatoes and washing other people's dishes, but nothing was too great a sacrifice for a chance to get to Texas, where he could begin his search for Charity.

Galveston was a bustling town in 1865. People were moving to the state in droves, many of them displaced Southerners who had lost everything. Towns sprung up all over and needed supplies, most of which were brought in by boat, and most of the boats were docking at Galveston to be unloaded. To Morgan, the town had a healthy spirit of adventure and renewal, almost a kind of renaissance. New buildings went up all over, and the traffic was like that of Memphis, but he thought the people were a little more polite and friendly.

As he walked along the wharf, he saw a sign on the side of a large freight wagon advertising for cross-country teamsters. He immediately looked the wagon master up and inquired about the position.

"I guess you can call me the wagon master," the leathery looking older gentlemen replied to Morgan's inquiry. "I own the wagons, so I guess that makes me the master."

"Sir, my name is Morgan Montgomery. I need a job, and I can handle horses or mules."

"I'm Zeb Tate. Ever handle a six-team hitch?"

"Yes, sir, on a farm back in Tennessee."

"I need men I can depend on, and you look dependable. We'll be leaving for Waco in a few hours, so stick around. The job's yours," Tate said, extending his hand for a handshake. "You'll do your own harnessin' and hitchin', so be here in about two hours to get your team ready."

"Mister Tate, I feel that I should tell you, I'm looking for a family who came out here a year or so ago. I want the job, and I'll drive your wagon to Waco, but I'll not likely stay with you after we get there. If that makes a difference, I'll understand."

"Young man, your kind of honesty is hard to find. You still have the job—pays five dollars a day and food. It'll take us seven or eight days with these heavy wagons. If it rains it'll take longer."

Morgan spent the two hours asking people about the McLaurens. He went to two livery stables, a land office, and several general stores, but no one remembered the family.

There were nine freight wagons in the convoy, plus a light wagon that carried the cooking pots and pans and enough food for the trip; it also carried feed for the animals. Zeb Tate and the cook driving the light wagon would get far enough ahead of the convoy to pick a camping place for the night and have food cooked when the heavy wagons arrived. The days on the bone-shaking Texas roads were long and exhausting. Morgan's first duty each night was to feed and tether his six horses. When that was completed, he would eat his evening meal, after which he would soon unroll his blanket under his wagon and bed down for a much-needed night's sleep.

As they passed through small communities and towns, Morgan would stop to ask if anyone had heard of a family named McLauren, but no one had. One night he said to his boss, "Mister Tate, I'm beginning to realize one thing: Texas sure is a big state."

Tate replied, "Boy, you ain't seen nothing yet. We'll only cover a small portion of Texas. After we get to Waco, you'd have to travel two hundred miles in almost any direction to get out of the state. If you're looking for somebody and don't know where to look, then you've got a big job cut out for yourself. And by the way, don't call me Mister Tate. Everybody calls me Zeb."

Shortly after they arrived in Waco, Zeb sent for Morgan to come to his office. "Morgan, I've been doing some thinking about your search for your friends. I've got wagons going out in every direction, even as far south as Corpus Christi. Why don't you consider staying around here and driving for me? I think you're a cut above most of my men, and I like you. I'll try to give you some of the long hauls, maybe try to send you in a different direction each time. That way you can ask about your friends while you earn a living."

Morgan had liked the older man from the first time he talked to him, back in Galveston. Zeb had many of the gentle qualities of John Newton, but like the Tennessee planter, he could be as hard as nails when the situation called for it.

Morgan stayed on with Zeb, driving the huge wagons wherever freight was needed. He traveled as far west as Amarillo and Lubbock. He even made a three-week drive to Corpus Christi and back. He traveled to Austin, Fort Worth, San Antonio, and many of the smaller towns scattered about over the state. Every chance he got he asked about the McLaurens, and each time he got the same reply—no one had ever heard of the family.

One day, after Morgan had been driving for him for about six months, Zeb invited him to supper at his house. Zeb's wife had passed away several years earlier, and he now lived alone in a large, white house at the edge of town. A Mexican woman named Lupe came in each day to take care of the house and cook for him. That night, Lupe had prepared a fine meal of pot roast with all the trimmings and oven-baked bread. Morgan couldn't remember when he had last enjoyed such fine food. After the meal they moved to the large living room at the front of the house and, at first, talked about mostly trivial things. But after a short while, Zeb's demeanor changed to a more serious look. "Morgan, you once told me you were from Tennessee, but I don't believe you ever told me what town."

"I grew up on a plantation near Columbia. I was orphaned at the age of nine, and a couple named John and Martha Newton took me in."

"Are they still living?"

"No, sir. They are both deceased. John died as the result of the war, and Martha died shortly after the war ended, when her home was taken away by carpetbaggers."

"That's too bad. So many people lost everything during the war, including me."

"You, Zeb?"

"Yes, I lost someone that meant the whole world to me. I believe Columbia is near Franklin, isn't it?"

"Yes, sir. It's about forty miles from my home—well, what *was* my home."

"My only son is buried near Franklin. He went to war with John Bell Hood. Got wounded at Stones River and later got killed at the Battle of Franklin. I don't have anyone left."

Morgan could see tears in the old man's eyes. "I'm truly sorry, Zeb." He wanted to say more but could think of nothing appropriate. There was a long silence before Morgan spoke again. "I was in the Battle of Franklin, sir."

Zeb wiped tears from his cheeks as he asked, "Was it really bad? I've heard stories."

Morgan didn't want to say more, but he had to answer his friend. "Yes, sir. It was awfully bad. We took a bad licking at that battle."

"What battle group were you with?"

"I rode with General Nathan Bedford Forrest."

Nothing else was said about the war, and after a few minutes, Morgan excused himself and left Zeb to his silent grieving.

During the next three years, Morgan traveled over most of Texas, delivering and picking up freight and always asking about the McLaurens. And as always, the results were the same. He never gave up trying, but hope was slowly fading.

One day Morgan came in from a trip, and Zeb wanted to see him. "Morgan, I want you to meet me here the first thing in the morning. We need to go to my attorney's office on some business. And please don't ask me anymore about it. I'll see you tomorrow."

Morgan couldn't imagine what kind of business Zeb had with an attorney that would require his presence. He had been helping with the scheduling and billing for the last two years, and he had brought in a lot of new customers, but none of that required an attorney.

Zeb was waiting in the office when Morgan arrived the next morning. They walked the two blocks to the attorney's office in silence.

"You are Morgan Montgomery?" the attorney asked, after Zeb and Morgan were seated across the large desk from the fat, middle-aged man.

"Yes, sir," Morgan answered.

"Morgan, I'm Tee Irvin Clayton, attorney at law. Zeb here is about to do something that, in my opinion, is extraordinary in this day and time, and something that speaks very highly of you. Zeb is giving to you, free and clear, one-half interest in his freight business."

Morgan was astonished and shocked at what he had just heard. He tried to speak, but the words would not come out.

"I thought you would be a little surprised as such news, but it's true," T. Irvin said.

Zeb said, "I've been considering this for a long time. You've helped build the business. I'm getting older, and I'm having a few health problems, so I need a good partner more than I need the money a partnership with someone else would bring in. And I don't know anyone else I would trust like I trust you."

"Zeb, I don't know what to say. I never, in my wildest dreams, expected something like this."

"I may not be doing you such a big favor, because you'll have to stay in the office a lot more, and that can drive an out-of-doors man nearly crazy."

T. Irvin Clayton came around the desk with a stack of papers. After pointing out several places for the two men to sign, he announced, "Well, it's done. Morgan, you are now half owner of the Tate and Montgomery Freight Line. I have a copy of the papers for each of you. I'll file a copy at the courthouse and retain one copy for my files."

During the next few years, new freight companies started up in the area, but before long they would go out of business. Tate and Montgomery, or T & M as they now went by, had such a reputation for honesty and dependability that no one could take business away from them. Morgan proved to be an astute businessman. Under his management the number of wagons grew to over fifty, with a branch office in San Antonio.

Morgan put all of his energy into the business, working all hours of the day and night. He had no family other than Zeb, who was now like a father to him, and there was no room in his heart for another woman. No one could ever replace Charity, and that was the way he wanted it. He talked to the single girls at church socials and would sometimes attend a community affair and dance with all the eligible girls, but things never went beyond talking or dancing. He often thought of Charity and still prayed that he would find her some day, although he realized the chances were growing slimmer each year.

In the spring of 1871, Zeb Tate died. His health had been failing the last few years, and Morgan had taken over all the duties of running the freight company. But Zeb's death was still a shock to Morgan, and he was deeply saddened by the loss. He seemed to lose everyone who mattered to him, and the experience never got easier. Zeb's funeral was held on the Sunday following his death. The church was packed with people from all over the state of Texas. Morgan made sure that Zeb's one request was carried out: he planted Zeb's favorite flowers on the grave, Texas bluebonnets.

He was so distraught over the passing of his dear friend and partner that he decided to get out of town for a few weeks. He left the business in the hands of a trusted assistant and headed south on his favorite saddle horse. His third night out he stopped at a roadside inn in the little village of San Marcos. The establishment was run by an amiable Mexican lady named Gonzales. Morgan was pleased with the tasty Mexican dishes. Several guests remained in the dining area after the meal to talk, but Morgan did not want to engage in conversation and retired to the patio. It was a pleasant place, with several large wooden chairs placed around a small cactus and rock garden. Some of the larger plants were in bloom, giving off a delicate, sweet fragrance. The western sky was beginning to take on a slight orange hue as the sun approached the horizon, and somewhere nearby he heard the peaceful mating coos of white-winged doves. This would be a good place to spend his evening until bedtime.

He had not been in the patio long before a young man came out, pulled a chair to one corner, and unfolded a newspaper. A few minutes later the proprietor came out and addressed the young man,

"Senor McLauren, it's good to have you back with us. I hope the food was to your liking."

Morgan did not hear the young man's reply. His heart was racing and beating so hard that he could hear his pulse. He stood up and looked at the other man. Yes, he did look familiar. Did he dare ask him his given name? Yes. "Sir, pardon me for intruding, but could you be Charles McLauren, from Mississippi?"

"Yes, I'm Charles McLauren. And whom do I have the pleasure of addressing?"

"Do you remember a wounded Confederate soldier recuperating at your home in the spring of sixty-three?"

Charles McLauren stood up and took a step toward Morgan. Then he stopped and paused for a moment before saying, "Morgan! Oh my God! Are you my sister's Morgan Montgomery?"

"Yes, Charles. I'm Morgan Montgomery, and you'll never know how long I've been searching for your family."

The two men embraced like long lost brothers, and Senora Gonzales quietly slipped away. The men stepped back, shook hands, and then embraced again. After a few minutes, they sat down to talk. Charles said that he was there to purchase a new bull, one of the English breeds that eastern farmers were so excited about, called Herefords. Morgan told Charles about living in Waco for the past eight years. When Morgan could stand the small talk no longer, he asked a direct question, "What about Charity? Is she all right? Is she ... well, please tell me about her."

"Charity is fine; she speaks often of you. She wrote letters to you during the war, and she sent letters to that town in Tennessee that you came from, but she never heard from you. She cried herself to sleep many a night. Morgan, she now believes that you're dead."

"I received several letters from her when I first went back to the fighting, and then they stopped. When I did get a chance to go back to Honeywood, I found everything totally destroyed. I could find no one who knew what had happened to your family. I went back a second time and found old Moses in Raymond. He could only tell me that the family had gone to Texas. I've been looking for Charity ever since the war ended."

"Morgan, I don't know how to tell you this, other than to come straight out with it, Charity is engaged to be married in two months. As I said, she believes that you were killed in the war."

A dull pain filled Morgan's chest, and his strength faded. He sat down again and bowed his head. *Oh Lord, please don't let this be true.* His whole world had just turned upside down—all of his plans, all of his dreams, and all of his hopes were instantly shattered.

Charles realized what a terrible shock the news had been to Morgan, and he remained respectfully silent until Morgan chose to speak. "I'm sorry, Charles. I've reacted very badly. I had no right to expect her to be waiting for me. Too many years have passed. Please tell Charity that I wish her all the happiness—tell her that I wish her a very long and happy marriage."

"She'll want to see you, Morgan. I know that she'll want to see you again. We live on a ranch near Castroville, a small village about thirty miles west of San Antonio. We went there to live with my father's Uncle Joseph when we were forced to leave Mississippi. I'm here on business, but I'll return tomorrow if you'll go with me."

"No, I don't think that would be a good idea. I'll not interrupt her plans after all these years."

"Believe me, she will want to see you. If you would feel better about it, let me go before you and tell her everything."

"I don't know … I want to see her, but I'm not at all sure that I could take seeing her while knowing that she's about to marry someone else. Let me think about it tonight, and I'll try to give you an answer in the morning."

Charles agreed and excused himself. Morgan stayed on the patio until well past dark. *Dear God, how many ways can a heart be broken? Must I always lose the ones I love?*

To Morgan's surprise, he fell asleep very quickly, and slept until sunrise. The burden of the long search was over, as well as the anxiety of not knowing. Before falling asleep, he had decided that he would not go to see Charity. She had her future ahead of her, and his appearance might confuse things. He also knew that his hurt and confusion would intensify if he were to be around her under those circumstances. He explained his position to Charles, telling his friend that he had decided to return to his home in Waco immediately.

CHAPTER 17

Afew days after Morgan returned to Waco, T. Irvin Clayton came to his office. "Morgan," Irvin began, "I have probated Zebedee Tate's will. Everything has been legally filed and recorded. Zeb has left his half of the freight business and his home to you."

Morgan was not really surprised. Zeb had often spoken about not having any living relative that he knew about and had told Morgan many times that he was like a son to him. He could not think of a reply to what the lawyer had just told him.

"He had nearly two hundred thousand dollars in his bank account, and he has left that to his church," T Irvin added.

"I'm glad of that," Morgan replied. "Zeb has been a very gracious contributor to the church for many years, and they might have experienced some financial difficulties without his support."

Spring faded as quickly as the bluebonnets and Red Indian paintbrushes, and a long hot summer was upon central Texas. Morgan went about his job with even more vigor and vitality than before. He would now have to make a new life for himself, a life without the dream of someday marrying Charity, and without Zeb's ever-present companionship and counsel. He moved into Zeb's house and retained Lupe as his cook and housekeeper. He began to occasionally entertain friends and even had a few dates with a lady school teacher who attended his church. He was not really happy, and he wasn't sure that he would ever be, but there was now a certain sense of well-being that had been absent from his life since he had left Oakmont for the war.

It was one of the hottest days of late summer. The sun beat down with an unyielding vengeance. The streets were barren of both man and beast, except for the unfortunate few who had to carry on the business of the growing town of Waco. Morgan was one of those few. For several days he had expected a letter from Washington containing contracts to haul freight to several outlying military installations. This would mean more responsibility for him, but it would also mean several more jobs for the people of Waco. After completing some pressing office chores, he braved the heat and walked the two blocks to the post office. He now employed two clerks and a bookkeeper, but he preferred to check the mail personally each day, regardless of the weather.

He received his mail while the postmaster engaged him in conversation about the unusual heat. Walking back on the shady side of the street, he took a quick look through the small bundle of envelopes, looking especially for the one postmarked Washington. His heart suddenly rushed as he observed the return address on one letter: *Mr. Charles McLauren, General Delivery, San Antonio, Texas.* He stopped in the shade of a live oak and opened the letter.

Dear Morgan,

I trust this will find you well. We are all well but Father; he spends most of his time in bed and refuses to eat properly. He will never get over the loss of Honeywood. We continually try to convince him that it was the war, and not his personal failure, that took away our Mississippi home.

Morgan, Charity has not yet married. When she learned that you were alive, she postponed her wedding. She now makes obvious excuses not to set a new date. I cannot say that she still loves you, but I know she is very confused about her true feelings for the man with whom she has been betrothed for two years.

I will now ask an immense favor of you. Please come to our home for a visit. I and my parents would like to see you, and Charity would not only like to see you, she needs to see you. She should either set a new date for the wedding or break the betrothal, and I do not believe she can do either without seeing you again. So, for her sake, and perhaps yours as well, please visit us soon.

Cordially yours,
Charles McLauren

The next morning Morgan boarded a stagecoach for San Antonio, a trip that would take two hot, dusty days. At times he was the only passenger onboard, which gave him ample time to ponder his situation in life. He practiced a sort of self-evaluation as he traveled.

He spent the first night of travel in the town of Austin because the stage had an all-night layover there. He had been to Austin several times during the past few years and had a favorite hotel where he always spent the night. At first the clerk told him that things were very busy in Austin; a lot of people were coming to town, and they had no room. Another employee came into the lobby at that time and saw Morgan. He immediately came over to Morgan and said with enthusiasm, "Mister Montgomery, what a pleasure to have you with us again."

"I was just told that you have no room for me," Morgan said.

"Nonsense," the man replied. "We always keep a room or two in reserve, and one of them is for you tonight. We'll always find a place for our special guests. Just sign in, and I'll make sure your room is ready."

Morgan was glad that the employee remembered him because he was too tired to go looking for another place to sleep. He went to his room to freshen up before going out for dinner. After eating a small portion of his meal, he decided to take a stroll around town. He no longer felt tired and he needed to stretch his legs after being cooped up in the rough-riding stagecoach all day.

The old section of Austin was small with board sidewalks and false-front store buildings, the kind he had seen in all the older towns around the country. Although it was well after dark, many of the stores were still open, and Morgan was surprised at seeing so many people on the streets. He saw a couple of saloons along the main street, with several horses tied at the hitch rails. He thought to himself that downtown Austin had probably not changed in the last fifty years.

There was a new section of Austin—the section where the town was growing, where all the newcomers and new merchants were building. Morgan did not leave the old section because he liked old things and old ways, and he was comfortable there. When he had walked several blocks, he felt that he could now sleep and headed for his hotel.

The stage departed just after sunup, and Morgan was pleased to be on the road again. There was only one other passenger, a man who didn't talk very much, which was fine with Morgan.

He tried to think of other things, but his thought always returned to Charity. Charles McLauren had asked him to come for Charity's sake, and regardless of the perplexity it might cause him, he must go to her. He could never refuse anything that might in any way benefit Charity. Although his love had become more bitter than sweet, his affection for the beautiful girl from Mississippi was boundless.

Upon arriving in San Antonio, he checked into the Cattlemen's Hotel to rest and freshen up. The intense heat had made the ride more exhausting than usual, and a hot bath and a good night's sleep worked wonders for his tired body.

The next morning he got to the livery stable by seven o'clock. He rented a large dapple gray stud, got directions from the stable owner, and headed west for Castroville. The gray quickly proved to be high-spirited; Morgan gave him his head and allowed it to run a couple of miles before taking control and slowing the animal down to a brisk canter. In the past few years Morgan had not taken time to ride much, and it felt good to be astride a horse again. He reached Castroville around three o'clock in the afternoon and stopped to ask directions to the McLauren ranch. He first asked an elderly Mexican man but could not make himself understood. He then went into a small general store and received directions and a big smile from the pretty Mexican girl who worked there. The girl walked outside with him and pointed out the road he should take, saying that it would be about a four-mile ride.

He had not been so close to Charity since the early summer of 1863, more than eight years before. How could his love be so strong after so long a time? His excitement grew with each passing mile. Would she look the same? Would she think he looked the same? What would he first say to her? Had Charles been right when he said that she needed to see him?

"Hold up there, mister! Get offa that horse." Looking into the late afternoon sun, he had failed to see the three riders stopped in the road ahead. He reined up his horse with one hand and lifted his free hand to shade his eyes from the direct sunlight, but failed to dismount. "Are you Montgomery?" someone asked in a gruff voice.

"Who wants to know?"

"I'll do the askin' around here. Just say if you're Montgomery or not."

"Yes, my name is Montgomery," Morgan replied, "But I'd sure like to know the name of the person who is so rude as to block the road and demand to know my name."

"Mister, you sure do talk fancy. All the name you need to know is Nick Slater. We work for him, and you ruined his weddin' plans. He'd be married to Miss Charity right now if you hadn't sent word to stop it. Now, turn that horse around and get back to where you come from."

"Listen well. I've been traveling two days, and I'm tired. I'm not turning around. I'm going to see the McLaurens, so move aside."

At that point, two of the riders spurred their horses and passed on either side of Morgan. As they passed, he got a quick image of a rifle butt coming toward his face. He saw tiny flashes of light just before everything went black. A moment later, he came to his senses enough to feel sharp pains as pointed-toe boots dug into his stomach and ribs. Then he heard, "Stop that! What are you doing to that man? You'll kill him."

"Mind your own business, old man, and get on down the road."

A second later he heard a loud boom of a shotgun. There was scuffing of men's feet as they ran, followed by the rapid hoofbeats of running horses. Morgan felt the coolness of water running over his face as a man's voice said, "Mister, you sure don't look so dandy. They worked you over pretty good."

It turned out that the good Samaritan lived on a small ranch near the McLaurens. He had been returning home from a business trip to town when he saw the three men beating Morgan and came to his aid.

When Morgan recovered enough to tell his rescuer where he had been going, the man helped him into his wagon and tied the gray to the back. It took a little over an hour of torturous bumping and swaying of the farm wagon to get to McLauren's ranch. Showing up in such a bloody and battered condition had not been the way Morgan envisioned his arrival, but there was nothing he could do. It was past sundown when the old man drove his team of horses up to the hitch rail and stopped. "Hello in the house," he called toward the long, low ranch house with a full-length porch. "Hello in there."

Charles came out first, followed by a young Mexican boy. "Hello, Mister Parker. What brings you over here?"

"I've got an injured man with me. Says he was coming to your place, so I brought him here."

"Has he been in an accident?" Charles asked as he walked closer to the wagon.

"No accident, unless you call three of Nick Slater's boys an accident. They was giving him what for when I come along. I fired off a round of buckshot, and they skedaddled."

"Hello, Charles," Morgan said as his young friend stopped a few feet from the wagon.

Charles hesitated, and then as he recognized Morgan, he advanced saying, "Oh! My God, Morgan. Oh my God!" He suddenly turned and ran into the house, leaving the young boy and the old man standing next to the wagon beside Morgan. In a moment he returned, followed closely by Charity. The moment had arrived that Morgan had waited eight long years for. He was actually seeing Charity again. Although she looked a little older than he remembered, she had grown more beautiful. A cool rush of emotion filled his breast and nearly took his breath away. His pulse raced, and he began to tremble as she came closer. Seated in the bed of the wagon, he leaned over the side and held out his hands. Charity started to take his hands but seemed to change her mind and embraced Morgan across the old wooden sideboard. He placed his arms around her and held her for several minutes.

"Oh, Morgan, I want to say so much, but I don't know where to start," she said after taking a step backward while sliding her hands along his arms until their hands touched.

"We need to get him inside and attend to his wounds," Charles said. "Then you'll have plenty of time to talk."

"What happened to you?" she asked. Before he could answer, she turned to Charles and demanded of him, "What happened to him? You said he had been hurt, but you didn't say how it happened."

"Some of Nick Slater's men stopped him on the trail and did this to him. I think they'dve killed him if I hadn't come along," Mr. Parked interjected.

"No! Not Nick! He would never have his men do something like this."

"Well, Miss Charity, I saw three of them beatin' and kickin' him. They hightailed it when I fired off my shotgun."

"How did they know he would be there, on the trail?"

"I'm afraid that's my fault, sis," Charles said. "I told Nick that I had sent for Morgan and expected him in a few days. I guess they've been watching for him."

"I saw one of them in the little store when I asked for directions," Morgan noted. "But I'd like to just forget about this and get cleaned up."

Charles and the Mexican boy, Pepe, helped him down from the wagon. With one on either side for support, they helped him walk into the house and to a large table in the kitchen. It was then that he saw another person he never thought he would see again, one of the people who helped nurse him back to health back in Mississippi. It was Sudie, the cook. "Why, Masser Morgan, I heard 'em call your name, and I was sho waitin' to see you. Lawdy, we heard you was dead, and we all cried. My goodness, you done gone and got yoself bad hurt again."

"Sudie, we'll need hot water and towels," Charity said as Morgan sat down on one of the chairs at the table. It was obvious to everyone that he was in great pain. "Oh, Morgan, you poor darling," Charity said as Sudie placed a pan of hot water and towels on the table. Those words brought a joy to his heart, although he wasn't sure they meant the same to Charity as they did to him. He was almost glad that he had such bad facial cuts and abrasions, because Charity spent the better part of an hour with her face in close proximity to his, cleaning away the dried blood and carefully doctoring each injury.

There was a knock at the front door just as she had finished her delicate work on Morgan. Charles answered the door and returned in a moment, followed by a tall, sun-darkened man who appeared to Morgan to be around forty years of age. "Nick, you have your nerve, coming here after your men did this to our friend," Charity said.

"Now, Charity, that's not fair," the new arrival answered. "I've come over to apologize to you—and to this man."

"This man," Charity replied, placing her hand on Morgan's shoulder, "has a name. His name is Morgan Montgomery. Nick, I never thought you would do such a thing."

"Dad blame it, Charity, if you'll just listen, I can explain everything. I didn't know anything about this until my foreman came in a little while ago and bragged about it. Said they did it for me. I gave him a piece of my mind before heading over here to set things straight."

"Go ahead, Nick, set things straight," she curtly replied. "See if you can say anything that will make Morgan feel better. See if you can make all the cuts and bruises go away."

"Mister Montgomery, I've been awfully upset at you, ever since Charity learned about you bein' alive and put off our weddin'.

Charity told me about you two years ago, but you didn't matter then, bein' dead and all. I guess I've had my bristles up ever since Charles come back here telling everybody that you was alive. I'm not about to change my feeling about you comin' here, but I'm real sorry about what my boys done to you. Guess I shouldn'tve mentioned to 'em that you was comin' here to cause more trouble."

Nick then turned to Charity and said, "I'll stay away while Mister Morgan Montgomery is staying here, as long as it's not too long. Then I'm aiming to get together with you, to get some things settled, like when we're gettin' married." With that he turned and walked out of the house.

Sudie took away the pan of bloody water and towels, and Morgan heard her say under her breath as she walked away, "Never did like that Masser Nick no how. Glad Masser Morgan done come."

"We'll be dining soon. Do you think you can eat? It might be difficult, with those cuts on your lip," Charity said.

"I'll fix him some good stew. Fed it to him fo' days back when ole Moses and Claude brung him to Honeywood," Sudie said as she gave Morgan her best smile.

"That won't be necessary," Morgan said. "I'm so hungry I don't think a split lip will keep me from eating." Charles showed Morgan to a spare room, where he groomed and changed into clean clothes.

When Morgan returned to the kitchen, he found Charles and Charity standing near the table where Charity had attended to his injuries. Seated at the table were Charlotte and Thomas McLauren; both looking old and tired, but there was a smile on each face in the room.

"Morgan, some eight or nine years ago I welcomed you to my home. This one is not so elegant as Honeywood, but you are still welcome," said Thomas.

"What Thomas said goes for me as well," Charlotte agreed. "You are always welcome in our home. I'm sorry I wasn't here to welcome you earlier, but I was with Thomas in his room and didn't know you had arrived."

The conversation during the meal was relaxed, with no one mentioning the war or the past. Thomas and Charlotte excused themselves as soon as the meal had been eaten, to return Thomas to his room.

"This is the first time in months that our entire family has eaten an evening meal together, and the first time Father has been out of his room in more than a month,"

Charles noted.

The good meal was followed by coffee and more trivial conversation. Then Charles said to Charity, "Why don't you take Morgan out to the veranda to talk for a while?"

"I would love to," she replied. Then addressing Morgan, she asked, "Do you feel well enough—I mean, should you get some rest?"

"Charity, I have the rest of my life to rest. I've waited eight years to talk to you, and I'm not about to let a little soreness come between us now," Morgan answered as he got to his feet and walked to Charity's chair to help her up. Charity took Morgan's arm and led him out of the room and out to the veranda, where they sat in an old wooden swing for a long time without talking.

Then Charity broke the silence. "I wanted to stay in Mississippi, close to you, but they convinced me that it wasn't safe for me, and they needed me. Both Mother and Father suffered such dreadful things at the hands of those soldiers. Morgan, you do understand why I had to come away, don't you?"

"Yes, I do understand. All of our choices were taken from us during that savage time. I lost everything that had any meaning, everything precious—my home, and both of the Newtons. And my greatest loss of all was when I lost you."

"Oh, Morgan, I'm sorry to hear about the Newtons. I know you loved them very much."

"Yes, I loved them like they were my parents. They took me in when I had no one else and treated me like I was their own child."

After that, they again became silent. Instead of talking, they listened to the night sounds, the distant lowing of cattle, the call of a night bird in nearby live oaks, and the gentle squeak of the swing. Morgan wanted to tell so much and to ask so much, but time had robbed him of the right words. The blissful contentment of just being with her, of finally being there by her side, took the place of conversation for him.

Finely, Charles came out of the house and broke the spell. "I came to say good night. I'm going to my room to read. I'll see you both at breakfast."

Morgan and Charity said good night to Charles, and he disappeared into the house. Then Charity said, "Morgan, I must tell you about Nick Slater."

"You don't have to do that, Charity. You see, I'm beginning to understand now that too many years have passed for me to expect things between us to be the same as they were back in Mississippi. That was a very emotional time, and you were so young. You fell in love with a young wounded soldier who was going back into battle. I had no right to hold on to all the dreams and expectations."

"Morgan Montgomery, you don't understand. Yes, I was very young—we both were. And yes, I did fall in love with you and was completely devastated when I stopped hearing from you. I cried myself to sleep every night for months, worrying about you, wondering if you had been killed or if you had just stopped loving me. I sent dozens of letters, but I only got a few from you, and that was soon after you went away."

"Charity, I've never stopped loving you. I wrote to you, but after a short time I stopped getting letters from you. I guess it was because we were always on the move. I returned to Honeywood the first chance I got, but I found only ashes and rubble, and you were gone. I asked about you, but no one could tell me anything. I went to Raymond later, and found old Moses. He told me what happened when the Yankees came, but he didn't know where you had gone. He remembered something about Texas. So I came to Texas as soon as the war was over, and I've been trying to find you ever since."

"Morgan, we finally decided that you were … well, that you had been killed. I still loved you very much, and I guess I still do, although I'm confused about my feelings. You know about my betrothal to Nick. Nick has been in love with me, or so he thinks, for several years. He's a very good man, a deacon in the church. He's always helping other people. He helped us with the ranch since we first arrived. Uncle Joseph died soon after we got here, and we knew very little about a cattle operation. We had raised cattle for milk and meat, but nothing on such a large scale as this ranch. Any time we needed help, Nick would send his men over to do whatever needed to be done. He even drove our cattle to market with his. If it hadn't been for that, we would have lost everything again. Charles has come a long way toward learning the ranching business, but we're not yet a successful ranching operation. It's been necessary to accept occasional help from Nick.

"I care for Nick, and I even thought I loved him. But everything changed that day Charles came home with the news that he had seen and talked with you. A lot of memories and a lot of forgotten feelings came rushing back. Nick changed after I asked him to postpone the wedding. He's always been such a gentle person, but lately he's become moody and temperamental. I'm a little frightened at the change in him. So you see, Morgan, I don't know what to do."

A slight breeze rustled the leaves of the old pecan tree that stood across the yard from the veranda. Morgan arose from the swing, took Charity by the hands, and gently pulled her up from the swing to face him. Eight years after two young lovers said good-bye with a lingering embrace and an amorous kiss, two older and wiser lovers said hello with a lingering embrace and an amorous kiss.

"Oh, Morgan, I do still love you, so very much."

"And I love you, my darling. I've never stopped loving you, not for one minute."

After another long kiss, they returned to their seats in the swing. Morgan's cut lips hurt from the pressure of the kisses, but he didn't care. The joy of being with Charity was greater than any pain he had ever experienced. He placed his arm around her, and she snuggled close to him. They sat there, cheek to cheek, for the better part of an hour before she reluctantly said, "It's getting late, Morgan. We should go in now."

"Yes, you're right, but I could stay here, just like this, forever."

CHAPTER 18

Morgan awoke to find the sun shining brightly through his bedroom window at such an angle that he knew it was late in the morning. He moved to get out of bed and instantly remembered the beating he had taken the day before. The exuberance over being with Charity had taken his mind off the hurting during the previous evening, but now almost every muscle in his body ached. He ambled over to the washstand and looked into the mirror. There was a smudge of dried blood on his lips where it had bled during the night. Both eyes were black and his cheeks were swollen. He washed his face in the large white basin and gently blotted the water away with a towel.

He dressed and went to the kitchen to find that Sudie was the only person there. "Good mornin', Masser Morgan. Got some food in the warmin' oven for ye."

"Good morning to you, Sudie. It appears that I've been a real sleepyhead, not getting up until so late."

"No, sah, you ain't no sleep-head. Miss Charity done tole me how y'all stayed up so late las' night. Now, jus' sit yoself down, and I'll fix yo breakfast."

Sudie first brought a large cup of steaming coffee and then followed with a blue willow plate loaded with ham, eggs, grits, and the kind of biscuits only she could make. "Miss Charity say to tell you she gone to Cast-o-ville with Masser Charles to get supplies. Say she knows you needs to rest, and she be back soon."

It was more difficult to eat this morning than it had been the night before with the bruised face and split lips, but he managed to consume almost everything on the plate. He couldn't remember having a breakfast that good in several years. As he finished his coffee, he engaged Sudie in conversation. "I was a little surprised at finding you here. Did anyone else come out here to Texas with the McLaurens?"

"You 'member Claude? He come with us, drove one of de wagons. He pass on 'bout two years ago. Masser Thomas put him right in the graveyard near Masser Joseph, say he's like part of the famly. He say I'm part of the famly too. Didn't have no room when we was comin' heah fo' any de udders. Ole Moses coulda come, and Masser Thomas woulda made room, but Moses say he be too old to go leavin' home."

"Well, I was sure glad to see you here. I know it means a lot to Charity and the rest of the family to have you with them. By the way, I saw Moses right after the war. He lives in a little house in Raymond."

"I sho is glad ole Moses got to stay close to home. I misses him more'n 'bout anybody we left behind." Sudie then stopped what she was doing and wiped a tear from her cheek with the corner of her apron. Then, with her best smile she said, "Masser Morgan, you sho be a lot nicer than Masser Nick. He never say anything nice to me. To tell the truth, he never talks to me at all."

"Thank you, Sudie. You are always a pleasure to talk with. It could be that Mr. Slater is a man of few words," Morgan replied.

He finished his coffee and walked outside to a beautiful sun-filled morning. There was no one in sight, and so he walked to the barn to check on the rented gray. There were signs that someone had recently fed the animal. He decided to saddle up and go for a ride around the ranch. In short order he was mounted and following a small road away from the barn. He stayed with it until it crossed a shallow stream lined with wild pecans and live oaks. There he turned away from the road and headed down one of the cattle trails that ran along either side of the meandering branch.

It was good to be in the saddle on such a nice day, with nowhere to go, no business to conduct, and no meetings to attend. There was time to think. He told himself that things would be different, now that he and Charity were reunited. There would be more to his life than running the freight business. He had accumulated a great deal of wealth, enough to last him and Charity the rest of their lives. He might even sell the freight line. In the last few years, several people had asked him to put a price on the total business, but he had never considered doing so. Now, a whole new world was opening up to him. He would never again have to bury himself in his work in order to ward off the melancholy and loneliness he had known for the past eight years.

He followed the stream for a couple of miles before turning to ride to the top of a high ridge so he could get a better idea of the lay of the land. He jumped long-eared rabbits, deer, and several bunches of long-horned cattle that bolted away faster than the deer. He wondered how anyone could ever hope to make a living with those wild, tough-looking cattle with horns as long as a man's arm. He had heard that many were being shipped from the port at Corpus Christi, and thousands of others were being driven overland to the railheads in Kansas.

There had been a strange-looking bull in one of the corrals at the barn, a large red animal with short legs and a white face. Morgan thought back to the day he had met up with Charles in San Marcos, when Charles had said he was there to purchase a Hereford bull. That big red had to be the one. Having grown up around all kinds of livestock, Morgan knew enough about cattle to know that it would take several generations of breeding to bring about enough change in those rangy cows to make them look like good beef cattle.

He topped the ridge and looked out across a vast, virtually unused wilderness of mesquite and scrub oaks. It was land that he believed would someday be cleared and made productive. But he wasn't sure it would take place during his lifetime. Texas truly had a lot to offer anyone who would be willing to work for it, but this land would not give up to productivity without a fight. Only those with patience and perseverance need apply for a future here.

The sun told Morgan it was near noon as he started back toward the ranch house. The cattle trail he followed zigzagged through thick stands of mesquites, causing him to occasionally become disorientated. As he rounded a bend in the trail, he came face-to-face with the three men who had given him the beating the day before. "Well, look what we have here, boys," said the one who had initiated the previous day's assault on Morgan. "We told you to turn around and go on back to wherever it is you come from, but I guess we didn't say it strong enough."

"You know what the boss had to say last night, Rowdy," the older of the three said. "Said we was not to bother him or even get near him."

"We didn't get near him. He's on Slater land, and that makes him a trespasser. That's the next thing to bein' a cattle thief."

"Count me out of this," the older man replied. "We done too much yesterday. I'm not gettin' fired just 'cause you want to whip this man again."

"Me neither," the third man joined in.

"Well, I guess I'll have to finish what we started yesterday, and I don't need no help," the one they called Rowdy said as he nudged his horse toward Morgan. Morgan had reined his horse to a stop as soon as he saw the three riders, and he had not moved during the conversation. He quickly summed up the situation, and surmised that trouble was coming, but it would only be between him and Rowdy.

"Mister, if anyone has a score to settle, it would be me. But I don't want trouble with you, so if you'll just let me pass, I'll forget about yesterday."

"I don't want you to forget about yesterday, and I don't think you'll ever be able to forget about what I'm fixin' to give you now." He reined his horse to one side and started a circle around Morgan.

Morgan didn't want trouble; he didn't want revenge. But he was not about to take another beating, if he could help it. He reacted with an old cavalry move that he had so often used during the war. He spurred the gray directly into the side of Rowdy's mount. Rowdy and horse went down. Morgan leaped from the gray and was upon Rowdy before he could get to his feet. Without the help of the other two, as he had had the day before, Rowdy proved to be an ineffective fighter and quite clumsy. The cowboy awkwardly charged again and again, and each time Morgan answered with a well-directed blow. In less than two minutes, the stunned and confused cowboy, covered with trail dust and blood, had been rendered unable to continue. His nose bled profusely, and both eyes were nearly closed as he mumbled to Morgan, "I've had enough."

Morgan spoke to the other two men, "Will you gentlemen please take care of this man? And when he's able to understand what you're saying, tell him that I didn't want this fight, and that I'm truly sorry that I had to hurt him."

"Mister, you've got nothing to apologize for," the older cowboy said. "We're the ones that ought to be apologizing to you, and I reckon that's what I'm a-doin' now."

"Apology accepted," Morgan replied. "I hope we can all just forget yesterday and today."

The two men dismounted and helped their defeated comrade to his horse. As they started to ride away, the older one turned his horse and said to Morgan, "Mister, I think I can speak for all of us, includin' Rowdy here: consider all of this forgot."

Morgan made his way back to the ranch and found that Charity and Charles had returned from Castroville during his absence. Charity came into the barn while he was unsaddling the gray. There was exuberance in her voice when she spoke. "Morgan, I hope you don't mind, but Charles and I have decided to have a real Texas shindig tomorrow night. We sent word to several families while we were in Castroville, and we've had some of our men ride to neighboring ranches with invitations. We'll have the hands cook a beef over an open fire pit, and we brought a woman and her daughter from Castroville to help Sudie with the other cooking. Oh, Morgan, we haven't done this since Uncle Joseph passed away. You don't mind, do you?"

"No, of course I don't mind. It sounds like a lot of fun, and I'd like to meet your neighbors."

"Morgan, you do understand that we had to invite Nick Slater. I'm afraid you might have the wrong impression of him, after what took place yesterday. But he's really a nice person, and he's done so much to help us with the ranch. I'd like for you to get to know him better."

"Charity, I could never dislike someone who has helped you and your family. Although I must confess, I'm quite jealous of him."

"Please, Morgan, try not to be jealous. I realized last night that I'm still very much in love with you. And I realize now that my feelings for Nick were of a platonic nature, feelings of strong friendship, but not the kind of love I have for you."

"Charity, you've just made me the happiest man in the world. I think my heart is about to burst from beating so wildly."

The two lovers moved toward each other, stopped inches apart, and then looked into each other's eyes until Morgan could stand it no longer. He took Charity into his arms and kissed her, long and tenderly.

The shindig was a real success. Guests started showing up by early in the afternoon and continued arriving until well after dark. The people were not dressed in their best clothes but in neat, clean everyday garments. The women wore sun bonnets, and the men all wore the wide-brim hats of which most Texans were fond. Most of the men and a few of the women wore pointed-tow boots. This was different from the get-togethers back at Oakwood, when the neighbors all wore their finest attire, even to an outside event.

They came from miles around to eat, dance, and visit with friends and neighbors that they hadn't seen for months, and in some cases even years. Most of the ladies gathered inside the house, where they could learn all of the latest gossip. The men got together in small groups on the big front porch or under some of the big trees that provided a cool late afternoon shade, discussing manly things like cattle prices or politics.

Morgan eventually met all the men and most of the women present. At times he grew a little nostalgic, remembering such events back at Oakmont before the war. But those quick moments of sadness were fleeting because he had so much to make him happy.

Thomas McLauren's physical condition seemed to have improved with the festivities. With Charlotte by his side, he circulated among the guests, laughing and talking and appearing much like Morgan remembered him back in Mississippi. Charity noted this fact as she talked to Morgan. "Just look at Mother and Father. I'm so happy to see them out and socializing with the neighbors. It's been a long time since I've seen Father this active. Maybe your being here, someone from the past, has something to do with it."

Morgan replied, "He still misses Mississippi, doesn't he?"

"Yes, very much. After all these years, he's not been able to adjust to life away from Honeywood."

Later, as the crowd began to wane, Nick Slater approached Morgan. "I'd like to have a word with you, in private," Nick said.

Morgan wasn't sure what Nick might have in mind, but nothing was going to spoil his ecstatic mood. By this time most of the ladies had joined the men folks outside. "Sure," Morgan answered. "Let's go into the house. I think everyone's out here, so that will give us some privacy."

"Morgan, I'm a practical man," Nick began when they found an empty room. "I'm deeply in love with Charity, but I've seen her happiness around you today. She don't have to hit me across the head with a mesquite club to let me know that she's still in love with you. I've had to compete with your ghost all these years, and I could handle that. But now you're here in the flesh, and I see her love for you, and I can't deal with that. I'll still do anything I can for Charity and her family, but I need to stay away from her for a while. Will you explain things to her and tell her that I can't bear to have her tell me she don't love me? Will you tell her that for me, tell her how it is?"

Morgan was deeply touched. This hard-fisted, weather-toughened Texan—who by nature of his success as a rancher, had surely faced and overcome some of life's most difficult challenges—now had tears welling in his eyes as he turned and walked away.

The last guest didn't leave until late, and so Morgan waited until the next morning to tell Charity about his conversation with Nick. When he had told her everything, Charity replied, "I'm truly sorry for him. I care for him, but I don't love him. I never wanted him to be hurt. Do you think I should go talk to him?"

"No. I believe seeing you would make things worse for him. Let it be. That's the way he wants it. They say that time heals all wounds, including a broken heart."

"It makes me sad to think that I'm the cause of someone as good as Nick having a broken heart. I do hope he will forgive me someday."

"There's nothing to forgive. I don't believe you ever encouraged him to fall in love with you."

"Oh, Morgan, I didn't. I always told him that I couldn't stop loving you. I believed that I would never see you again, and that gave him hope that I might love him someday. And I guess I do love him, but only like a brother, like I love Charles."

"Charity, you've told me that you still love me. Now, will you tell me that you will marry me?"

"Oh, Morgan, yes, I'll marry you. Yes, yes, yes!"

"Charity McLauren, at this moment, I think I'm the happiest and luckiest man alive. I suppose it's time for us to talk about our future plans. Things like, well, where we'll live."

"I'll go anywhere you want to live. We can live in Waco, or we can live here, or any other place you choose."

"What about your mother and father?" Then he added, "And Charles?"

"Charles will always be here, on the ranch. He's quite intent on making it a successful operation. He loves this wild country, and he has changed so much since we came to Texas. Mother and Father will want what is best for me, and that means being with you, wherever you choose. The only place Father would ever be truly happy is back in Mississippi, and that can never be. During the times he feels like talking to us, it's always about Honeywood and the good times back there. And I miss it too. I had to stop allowing myself to think about our home; the memories used to put me in a melancholy mood for days. I'm sorry, darling. I didn't mean to get on that subject. To answer your question, I'm sure they will spend the rest of their lives here."

"Is there any reason to delay getting married?" Morgan asked.

"I only need enough time to make the arrangements, maybe a month. There'll be a dress to make, invitations to send out, food to prepare, and a thousand other things I can't think of right now."

"I have to go away on business," Morgan said. "It might take me as much as a month, or even a little longer. So, why don't we set the date for six weeks from now?"

"Six weeks will be fine with me. Oh, Morgan, I can't believe this is finally happening to me, after all the years!"

"Neither can I, my love, but it is really happening. I'll never let anything come between us again. All I want in life, from this day forward, is to make you happy."

CHAPTER 19

Five days later Morgan was in the office of T. Irvin Clayton. He had arrived back in Waco the morning of the previous day and had spent the afternoon catching up on business activities that had taken place during his absence. He now had important matters to discuss with his attorney. He was selling the freight business. There had previously been an offer by a group of businessmen to buy the thriving enterprise, but Morgan had not been interested. Now he was. He gave T. Irvin authority to contact those men to see if the offer was still valid. If so, T. Irvin was to draw up all the necessary papers.

Within a week, agreements were signed, but due to the large amount of capital involved, Morgan had to allow the group a month to raise the full amount.

In a letter to Charity, he explained that his business was taking a little longer than he had expected and asked if she would mind postponing their wedding by two weeks. He felt a new kind of loneliness and missed Charity more than he had ever missed her during the long years since the war. He wanted to go back and be with her during the time it would take to close the deal, but he had far too much to do before the wedding. During the stagecoach ride back to Waco, he had come up with a plan to give Charity the very best wedding gift possible. It would involve a great deal of money, but it would make her, and the rest of the family, very happy.

In less than two weeks, T. Irvin informed Morgan that the purchasers had gotten all the necessary funds and that they were ready to close the deal. That was exceptionally good news to Morgan, because he would now have extra time to prepare for Charity's surprise gift. Six days later, Morgan was on a boat out of Galveston, bound for New Orleans. He carried a letter of introduction from his banker with authority to draw funds from his personal account.

Morgan encountered several delays in his secret project, but he managed to complete his task and get to the McLauren ranch on the morning of the day set for his wedding. He had not expected a big turnout, but when he arrived at the ranch, the corral was full of horses, and a dozen animals were tied at the long hitch rail in front of the house. There were several light wagons, buggies, and carriages parked in the open space between the house and barn.

One of the ranch hands spotted Morgan as he approached the complex, and the word quickly got to Charity, who ran to him with open arms as he dismounted. "Oh, darling, I know we are not supposed to see each other before the ceremony on our wedding day, but I simply had to see you. I've missed you so very much. Time passed so slowly while you were away," she whispered as she placed her arms around his waist and held him with all her strength.

"I've missed you, too," Morgan told her, "more than I can ever put into words. But we'll never have to be separated again, not for anything."

"Morgan, I've been looking for you for a week, and when today came and you were still not here, I was about to go into a state of panic. I was beginning to visualize all kind of things happening to you. But you're here now, and we'll soon be married. Nothing can spoil this day for me. Nothing."

"My precious Charity," Morgan replied, "Although I've lost my faith a few times during the past eight years, my prayers are surely being answered today. With you by my side, I'll never lose my trust in God again."

The wedding took place at three o'clock in the afternoon. Charity and Charlotte had planned for the ceremony to take place in the spacious parlor, but there were too many people present to get into the house, and so they moved everything out to the large front porch. Those who couldn't find a place on the porch could still observe the marriage service from the yard. The porch was lavishly decorated with colorful floral arrangements. Several ranch hands and some of their wives had spent the morning gathering and arranging wild flowers, and the neighbor women had brought many bouquets of their favorite domestic varieties. Even the numerous prickly-pear cactus plants that persistently grew near the house were in full bloom.

"Friends and neighbors, we are gathered here today for a very joyous and happy occasion," the old preacher began. "We are about to see this man, Morgan Montgomery, and this woman, Charity McLauren, joined together in holy wedlock." Then he opened an old, leather-bound Bible and read from it. "*But from the beginning of creation God made male and female. For this cause shall a man leave his father and mother, and cleave to his wife; and the twain shall be one flesh; so then they are no more twain, but one flesh.* That was from the book of Mark, chapter ten, verses six through eight. Folks, marriage is one of the most wonderful institutions God ever ordained. I've talked considerable with Morgan and Charity this afternoon, and I believe that they too realize how beautiful marriage can be, otherwise I don't think we would be here today."

He stopped talking for a moment, pulled a folded handkerchief from his pocket, and wiped large drops of perspiration from his brow. "Morgan and Charity realize the responsibilities they're about to take on—the responsibility of being helpmates to each other, and of providing spiritual guidance to the children that come from this union."

The old preacher then turned to face Morgan and Charity. "I don't have a lot of fancy words to say. I believe in a simple Christian ceremony. Face each other, and Morgan, take both her hands in yours." When this was done, the old preached continued, "Do you, Morgan, take Charity to be your lawfully wedded wife, to cherish and to protect, in sickness and in health, and to keep yourself unto her only, till death do you part?"

"I do."

"Do you, Charity, take Morgan to be your lawfully wedded husband, to cherish and to hold, in sickness and in health, and to keep yourself unto him only, till death do you part?"

"Oh, yes, I do."

"I now pronounce you man and wife. Morgan, you may kiss the bride."

Promises made so long ago and so far away had now been kept. As Morgan kissed Charity Montgomery, he remembered that parting kiss during a bitter war, back in a rose gazebo on a plantation in Mississippi, and he thought, *Miracles still happen.*

It took the better part of the next hour for all the congratulations and best wishes to be said. Charles came to Morgan and gave him a manly hug as he said, "Morgan, I am so proud to have you as a brother-in-law. You've made my sister so happy." Morgan was surprised to see tears in his eyes as he turned and walked away.

Sudie came out of the house and approached Morgan. "You sho lookin' at a happy ole woman, Masser Morgan." She put her arms around him and put her head against his chest, and he embraced her tightly. After a minute she pulled back and said, "Masser Thomas had ta go inside to rest, but he say for you to come see him."

Morgan found Thomas sitting in the parlor. The older man began by saying, "I'm thoroughly exhausted. I had to come in to rest, but I wanted to tell you what's on my mind. Morgan, my boy, I want to first welcome you into our family. I can't begin to tell you how pleased I am that you and Charity found each other again, and how happy I am for the two of you. I can rest at ease now, knowing that Charity is truly happy."

At that time Charlotte came into the room and immediately came over to Morgan. "I don't mean to interrupt your conversation, but I just had to give you a big hug and tell you how happy I am. So many years have been wasted, but you two are together now, and that is all that counts."

Charity came into the parlor after she managed to get away from all the well-wishers outside. "Oh darling, my heart is about to burst, I'm so happy. The Bible says that God works in mysterious ways, but now he has brought us together, now and forever." She took him by the arm as she said to her mother and father, "I need to take him back outside; a lot of folks are asking for him. We can all talk later."

The wedding guests were then treated to food and music, Texas style. Two long tables and one small one had been set up under two old pecan trees that stood across the yard from the main house. All through the night and morning, two of the older Mexican ranch hands and several young boys had been meticulously cooking a calf, two yearling deer, and a half dozen young pigs over pits filled with glowing embers of mesquite logs. Sudie used all the cooking skills developed during thirty-plus years of cooking for the McLaurens to produce a table full of cakes, pies, and a variety of cookies and custard desserts. As guests from far and near heaped their plates with the fine food, a mariachi band from San Antonio played soft Spanish music.

By nightfall all the guests had departed. At Morgan's request, Charity and the McLauren family joined him in the parlor. "Folks, this has been, without a doubt, the best day of my life," Morgan began. "God has blessed me by giving me Charity for a wife. And you, Mother and Father McLauren, have honored me by accepting me into your family. Now, I want to do something to show my appreciation for all the wonderful things that are happening to me. Charity, we talked about where we might live after the wedding, but we never came to a definite decision."

"Darling," Charity said, "I knew you would make the right decision for all of us, and I was glad to leave such plans in your capable hands."

"Thank you for the confidence. I have made plans, and I only hope that, with God's help, I've made the right plans, because they include not only the two of us, but Mother and Father McLauren as well. Charles and I talked about this a couple of months ago, before I returned to Waco to settle my business. He told me that he planned to stay here on the ranch, regardless of what the rest of the family decided to do. He feels that this is where he will be able to prove himself, by continuing to build a successful cattle breeding operation.

"I like living in Waco, but you've never been there, and you might not like it at all. I really like this area, and I admire the fine people who live around here, but I'm not sure I would want to live here the rest of my life. I tried to think of a place where we would all be happy, and I believe I found just the place." He paused for a moment, as if trying to find the right words. "As we were saying our vows today, a contractor and his carpenters were busy building a new but very familiar home." Morgan then walked across the room to where Charity was seated. He removed an envelope from his coat pocket and handed it to her. "This is my wedding gift to you."

Charity opened the envelope, removed and unfolded an official-looking paper, and began to read. In a moment she exclaimed, "Is this … I mean, is it true? Is this really what it appears to be?"

Yes, my love. You're holding the deed to Honeywood. The war turned that beautiful, glorious place to ashes, but from the ashes of glory we'll build our future, and a future for our children, however many there may be.

Very little had to be done before leaving for Mississippi. Morgan had worked diligently during the weeks preceding the wedding to make sure the trip would be worry-free for his new bride and her parents. Charles had reaffirmed his desire to stay in Texas and work the ranch. Thomas and Charlotte were overjoyed by the knowledge that they would be going back to Mississippi, and when asked if she wanted to return to their old home, Sudie was only able to say, "Yes! Oh Lord, yes," after which she began to weep openly.

There would be no need to take anything but personnel belongings, because Morgan had commissioned a Jackson merchant to purchase and deliver complete furnishings for the new home, the kind of furniture that had once graced the stately McLauren home. The merchant had been instructed to spare no expense.

On the day of departure, Charles drove the travelers to San Antonio in a carriage, which was followed by a light wagon with their luggage, driven by one of the ranch hands. The stagecoach to Galveston would not depart until the next morning, so they took rooms for the night in a hotel near the stage station. The next morning, shortly after a hearty breakfast at the hotel dining room, Charles told everyone good-bye and returned to the ranch, and the five travelers boarded the stage.

The stage ride to Galveston was tiring and uneventful, but the two-day boat trip to New Orleans was pleasant and relaxing, even for the five people who were very eager to get to their destination. Morgan purchased a large covered wagon and a stout team of horses in New Orleans, and after two days shopping and buying supplies, they were on their way home.

That year, 1873, Morgan and Charity Montgomery, Thomas and Charlotte McLauren, and Sudie, along with a host of guests, celebrated Christmas in a grand new house, built almost identical to the old one, on a plantation called Honeywood.